# REAWAKEN

UNDER MY SKIN, BOOK #2

CHRISTINA LEE

Published by Christina Lee

Cover design by Kanaxa

Editing provided by Keren Reed. Proofing completed by Lyrical Lines and Judy's Proofreading.

# BLURB

Losing his adoring husband shattered Tristan Rogers's world. For the past few years, he's been going through the motions, running their dog grooming business while hiding the loneliness he feels down to his bones. When he witnesses an ugly breakup between a pretentious customer and his boyfriend, Tristan can't help but intervene. Something about the unassuming younger man calls to him, and he can't help wondering if he's experienced some heartache of his own.

Life took a tragic turn for Jonas "West" Hollis as a teen, and he's felt indebted to his overbearing lover ever since. Tristan's kindness draws him from the start, but with his dreams finally in reach, West can't risk getting close to someone else. Not now that he can live his life and stand on his own merit.

From innocent texts to companionable rides on Tristan's boat, what starts as an unexpected friendship between the men sparks into undeniable attraction. Neither are ready for anything deeper than a couple of passionate nights wrapped in each other's arms but their connection becomes too intense for either to ignore. If Tristan and West want to heal their broken hearts, they'll need a considerable amount of trust and courage—not only in themselves, but also each other.

*For Rob. I'm thrilled you got a second chance at love. I wish you a lifetime of special, happy, magical moments.*

# 1

# TRISTAN

I FLIPPED THE SIGN ON THE DOOR TO CLOSED AT DOGGIE STYLES, the dog grooming and day-care business I'd owned for the past eight years. It was our late night of the week, when we stayed open until seven. I had just gathered the receipts on the counter when the last customer walked through the entrance, the bell above the door jangling. Glancing over my shoulder, I bristled, even though I knew exactly who the owner of the two remaining dogs was. It was the customer we referred to as Mr. V—which stood for Voldemort—because of his combative and sanctimonious attitude.

"Cool, we're just about to close up shop," I remarked in a steady voice, when I really wanted to tell him that it was about *damn time*.

After he grunted in my direction, which was standard for him, I couldn't help glancing toward the parking lot, where Mr. V's younger boyfriend sat in the car parked on the far end of the small lot. I could barely make him out except for the black hoodie that seemed to engulf him and that he wore on regular rotation, whether purposefully or not. I didn't know why I was so intrigued by him; maybe it was more so because of his relationship to Mr. V.

They seemed like such opposites—Boyfriend's worn hoodie versus V's crisp, dark suits—but I supposed that wasn't anything new.

My late partner, Chris, and I also had vastly different interests, but we seemed to work, had even opened this business together. I had met him when I was only eighteen and just coming out, and we had become fast friends first before falling helplessly in love a couple of years later. Guess you could say we'd been together ever since—until he died almost three years ago from brain cancer.

While I was snapping the leashes on V's two six-year-old sibling pugs, named Coco and Chloe, V shifted around uncomfortably, like he was in a rush. He glanced at his shiny silver watch as if I was infringing on *his* time, so I moved slower to spite him. Self-important people were frustrating as hell, which was another reason why the boyfriend fascinated me—he seemed humble in contrast. Though he didn't speak much the couple of times he'd picked up the pugs, and only once did I notice him smirking about something my employee Elijah had said, which made me wonder if he had an equally sarcastic sense of humor.

I watched V head to his expensive blue German car as my employees finished disinfecting the floors on the day-care end. We kept this place squeaky clean—a requirement of any business in the service industry, but with animals, who could spread kennel cough or any other contagious illness like wildfire, hygiene was mandatory.

We'd recently become paperless, or at least we were trying to, so I began scanning the receipts into a computer program Elijah had talked me into. As it turned out, he was great with record-keeping methods—go figure—and I was grateful for it; we'd sort of been a mess since Chris passed away. I glanced up just as Brin and Brooke removed their plastic gloves and threw them over the sink basin to dry. "Are we all good?" Brin asked.

My dog, Mack, a corgi-sheltie mix, nudged at my ankle

beneath the desk, where he lay on a cushion. He was nine years old, and the energy at the day-care was too much for him most days, so when I brought him to work with me, he normally stayed underfoot and was always pretty chill.

"Yep. I'll get the trash," I replied, tipping my head toward the large black garbage bag we used toward the end of every day. "Have a good night."

"See you tomorrow," Brin replied, and I waved in their direction as they headed out the door. Those two had been goofy all day today, and it warmed my heart. Brin, blissfully happy with his new boyfriend, Nick, and Brooke, with her stories about her husband and kids, made our little family here complete. If there was one thing I felt settled about, it was that I had chosen good employees I could trust to get me through some rough times.

I got lost in methodically cleaning up the mess of paperwork spread across the desk, dragging my feet about going home to an empty apartment. It was lonely without Chris, but as the weeks and months went by, that bone-deep sorrow had abated a touch and became my new normal. The pain never really went away; you just learned to live with it.

I'd considered moving because so much of Chris was still inside that place, but I just didn't have the energy to think about it most days. I had bagged up his clothes and donated them to charity in the weeks after. Chris would've rolled his eyes at me because that was my usual MO. I didn't hold on to most things for too long. I was always cleaning out this or that, and I supposed I could blame my upbringing in the foster care system for that. Everything I owned was always reduced to one garbage bag as I moved from place to place.

Thing was, I figured if his stuff was gone, the sorrow would be too, but it didn't work that way. Besides, his family was a constant reminder of the life we had shared. We still got together every holiday and reminisced about Chris—it was as much a comfort as it was painful. But I was tied to them in so many ways, and I couldn't let that go, not yet, maybe not ever. My fingers moved absently, methodically swiveling my wedding ring, which I also couldn't seem to part with, let alone remove, three years later.

After making myself a to-do list for tomorrow, I headed out the door with the trash, and Mack on a leash. I secured the bolt behind me, then froze in place for a split second, shocked to still see Mr. V's car in the empty lot.

The windows were apparently cracked because their raised voices were carrying across the asphalt, and it sounded like they were in the middle of an argument. I attempted to mind my own business as I lifted Mack to the back seat of my truck and then headed toward the large Dumpster at the corner of the lot that all the establishments in the plaza used.

I lifted the lid, threw in the bag, and just as I turned toward my truck, V's boyfriend suddenly exited the car in a huff.

"You need to let me go and just...give me some space," he said and slammed the door, pulling his worn backpack over his shoulders. It looked sort of heavy, like it was crammed with a bunch of things.

He glanced at me briefly and narrowed his eyes in challenge as he adjusted the hoodie over his head. He was obviously fired up, and I certainly did not want to get caught in the crosshairs. So I put my head down and moved my feet toward my truck.

When Mr. V stepped out of the vehicle, my gaze stayed pinned to him; I couldn't look away even if I tried.

"Get back in the car," he said in a commanding voice that made me bristle. "We'll talk about this at home."

"No," Boyfriend said. "I told you, I'm done. You can keep everything—it's all in your name anyway." He fished his phone out of his pocket and threw it through the open passenger side window.

The statement threw me. Was V a controlling bastard?

*None of my business*, I told myself and sank behind the wheel of my car. Except, even though I turned the key to start the engine, I couldn't seem to make myself move. Instead, I slowly cracked my window to listen for anything distressing.

"It'll be better. I promise." The tortured sound of V's voice carried, and for a split moment I almost felt bummed for him. I had never heard him anything other than gruff. "We can work something out. I can give you what you need."

Boyfriend growled in frustration. "That's the problem; don't you get it? I need my own life." Boyfriend began walking away, and V followed him onto the sidewalk, near the crosswalk. There was a noticeable height difference between them, but both were on the lean side. V grabbed for his boyfriend's arm, and there were clipped words being said between them in a hushed tone.

My heart thrashing in my chest, I thrust the car in reverse and pulled out of the space toward the street. They were still going at it, V gripping his boyfriend's sleeve, and apparently sheer adrenaline coupled with frustration compelled me to take action. Nobody should be guilted out of needing space and time.

I pulled alongside the pair and shouted through my unrolled window. "Get in."

Both sets of shoulders stiffened as they gaped at me.

"Huh?" Boyfriend asked in a puzzled voice.

"I said, get in the goddamn car." Holy shit, what the hell had come over me?

"What the fuck are you doing?" V asked as the boyfriend's jaw dropped open.

"Making sure this doesn't lead somewhere you'll regret later," I bit out as I stared at the grip he had on his lover's arm. Understanding my point, V released his hold.

Boyfriend let out a breath and used the opportunity to take a wide step back.

I narrowed my eyes at V. I had a slight weight-and-size advantage and could take him on if I needed to.

"Get in," I said again, and Boyfriend's eyes met mine. They were dark and stormy, matching the color of the bangs that lay disheveled on his forehead. "He won't follow you, not if I have anything to do with it. I'll take you wherever you need to go."

Boyfriend hesitated a brief moment before he calmly walked to the passenger side door, opened it, and slid inside my truck. His scent filled the car, and I recognized the aroma immediately because Chris's mother loved cooking with rosemary. He finagled his overstuffed backpack between his knees on the floor, and again I wondered what in the hell he had inside there.

I drove away without a moment's hesitation, not wanting to give V enough time to walk back to his car, jump in, and follow us. But when I glanced into the rearview mirror, V still stood on the sidewalk, shoulders slumped, looking shocked and defeated.

## 2

## TRISTAN

"You did the right thing," I remarked as I turned down the closest side street, heading toward the freeway, not really sure which direction to go.

Boyfriend slumped down in the seat, his face shielded by his hood, but I heard him release breath after breath. I'd bet his pulse was going just as crazy as mine was right then. What the hell had I gotten myself into?

"Where to?" I asked, making sure he didn't feel trapped in the car with me.

He finally glanced my way, his gaze filled as much with trepidation as wonder.

After another beat he still didn't answer me, only casually shrugged one shoulder.

Fuck, he didn't have anywhere to go. I'd admit, at first I thought he'd planned that little display with V, but probably not, given the brief hint of fear in his gaze before his jaw clenched with a quiet determination I admired.

"It's okay," I said. "I've got an idea."

He didn't speak, only glanced out the window at the passing landscape, his fingers tapping on his knee like a nervous tic. He was probably having second thoughts about what he'd done. But in my mind, it was brave. Especially if I'd heard that snippet of terse conversation between them correctly. It sounded like at the very least, Boyfriend needed some time to think.

A few tense minutes later, I veered my car into the lot of my apartment on Lake Avenue. I was on the twelfth floor with a direct view of Lake Erie, and honestly, I wouldn't want to live anyplace else. It was a sight you didn't ever quite get used to.

"What are you doing?" Boyfriend blinked rapidly as I cut the engine.

"This is my place," I replied, cracking open my door.

"I don't even *know* you." He sounded a cross between bewildered and offended. I'd bet he definitely gave V a run for his money. And the whole time, my imagination had dreamed up this sweet, timid guy, who fell on the passive side. You know what they say about assumptions.

"You know me well enough." I shrugged. "I own a grooming business. I take good care of your dogs a couple times a week."

When he didn't reply, I got out of the car and briefly poked my head back inside. "You can stay overnight on the couch if you need to figure something out. Or you can leave. No pressure either way."

Once I began trudging up the footpath with Mack in tow, I heard the car door slam behind me as he followed me up the walk. I couldn't contain the small smile that traced my lips. We were silent as we strode through the lobby and into the empty elevator. I could feel his gaze on me as I punched the number and we rode up to the twelfth floor, like he was either reconsidering his decision or attempting to figure me out.

After we got inside, I led him through the narrow hallway past my bike, which hung neatly on a couple of pegs to save space. I wordlessly fed Mack and then pulled out leftover pizza and reheated a couple of slices for the both of us. When I handed him a plate he nodded in thanks, eating in silence as he stood in front of the wall of windows, glancing out at the dusky lake illuminated by the city skyline. It was a gorgeous view, and by the way he inched closer to the glass, I could tell he was as taken by it as I was the first time Chris showed me the place ten years ago. *Jesus, what have I gotten myself into, Chris?*

*About damn time you took some action,* he whispered back. He was always up for some kind of adventure. The exact reason we opened Doggie Styles, even though I never thought it would amount to anything other than a pipe dream. But as I watched Boyfriend stare into the dark night, I was reminded just how complicated people and their relationships were. Animals were easy in comparison. Their needs were simple, their love unconditional. I preferred their company during the hardest of times.

Shaking my bleak thoughts away, I reached for clean sheets from the linen closet and made up the couch. He sank down heavily on the cushion, and for the first time, it was evident how exhausted he was. Noticing the dark circles beneath his eyes, I questioned whether this decision had been a long time coming and if he now regretted the effort it had taken out of him. Mack nudged his fingers with his nose, and he stroked him dotingly on the snout and behind the ears. His gentle touch was endearing, and I wondered if he missed the pugs. When Mack was satisfied, he lumbered over to his pillow in the corner of the room to lie down.

Boyfriend's hands slid to his hood, and he slowly peeled it back. I held my breath when all this dark, fine hair bounced out —messy, and the length of his bangs fell in line with his cheekbones, which were dotted with faded freckles. Against the soft glow of the table lamp, his jaw looked chiseled, and his eyelashes were the longest I'd seen on a man as they curled against his lids and framed his soft brown eyes. He leaned over to pull his backpack toward him and began rummaging through it. At first glance I immediately noticed a rolled-up shirt, a pair of jeans, and an open envelope of money. Maybe he hadn't planned on leaving V tonight but had stashed the clothes and cash just in case.

*None of my business.*

I didn't want him to feel like I was watching him, so I hit the kitchen light and began loading the dishwasher. Next I folded laundry while watching a cooking show. He seemed to perk up when I changed the channel to the Food Network to tune in to a show I religiously watched called *Chopped*. I wondered if he liked cooking and that was why he smelled like rosemary. But it just as well could've been his shampoo.

I shelved the folded towels in the linen closet and then stretched my arms to the ceiling, the long day having taken its toll. He wasn't the only one who was beat.

"The bathroom is that door on the left," I said, motioning to the short hallway. "Feel free to rummage around for anything to eat or drink if you're still hungry. I'm going to hit the hay."

"Th...thank you," he replied in a throaty voice, dragging his gaze away from the television. "For helping me out."

It was the first time he'd spoken since he'd arrived at my apartment, and I questioned whether he was always that quiet or only in front of strangers. Or maybe his voice had grown quieter the longer he was with V. It happened, but I was more than likely being dramatic.

"No worries. If you need to borrow a phone, my landline is in the kitchen," I said, probably sounding my age. Did anybody use anything other than smartphones nowadays? But at the time, Chris had insisted we keep it. Besides, Boyfriend and I weren't *that* far off, were we? I was thirty-eight, and I was going to guess he was around twenty-four, give or take a year or two. I supposed in his eyes, I was already nearing retirement. And some days I even felt like it. Jesus, listen to me.

At the door of my bedroom, I asked, "Do you have a name?"

"Huh?" His brow furrowed as his gaze swung from the cooking show, where the chef was sautéing onions.

"Your name?" I reiterated, feeling like it was a pretty easy question, given the fact I was allowing this virtual stranger to sleep on my couch. Christ, I wasn't asking for his family history or anything. "I'm Tristan."

He paused a beat. "Um...West. My name is West."

"*West*," I echoed, testing the syllable in my mouth. I had wondered for so many months. "You're safe here."

His eyebrows rose to his hairline. "It's not what you think. Michael...he's not *hurting* me. He's just...*overwhelming*, and I..."

"You don't need to explain to me." I held up my hands, kicking myself for saying anything at all. The name Michael sounded way kinder than Voldemort. Maybe we'd been too tough on him. Except, it was hard to mistake his constant gruff demeanor. "Good night."

I urged Mack off his pillow to follow me inside my room, thankful I had taken him for a walk on my lunch hour earlier in the day. But before I closed my door, I looked back at West one last time. He seemed so lost and forlorn as he stared in my direction. "If you need to borrow anything at all...feel free. All yours."

In the morning West was gone. And so was my bike.

---

ELIJAH WAS ALREADY AT DOGGIE STYLES WHEN I ARRIVED THE following morning. We moved around each other in silence, both still tired and needing more coffee. He started the machine on the rolling cart we kept at the back corner near the sink and small fridge, and once it got brewing and the smell filled the space, I instantly felt more alert.

I'd had a restless night of sleep with West in the next room, yet I still didn't hear him leave my apartment, let alone with my bike in tow. Neither did Mack, so we'd both be hopeless against a burglar, apparently. Still, the idea of it made me grin like a fool.

I *did* tell him he was free to borrow anything.

And here I'd pictured this young guy who cowered before V's grumbly and controlling exterior, but what I'd witnessed yesterday was anything but. He'd stood up to him and had fended for himself, and given V's sadness about their parting, there was way more to their relationship than I had given it credit for.

I should've known better—relationships were always complicated.

When I handed Elijah the cup, he still didn't look his cheerful self. "You okay?"

"Yeah, sure," he replied, sipping the black liquid. "Had an argument with Stewart last night."

Their quarrels seemed to be numerous, now that the honeymoon phase was over. Relationships were tough, and you usually needed to be on the same page in order to work most things out.

"You know you can talk to me about anything, right?"

He nodded. "I just hate when he pulls the silent treatment on me. It's so…"

"Juvenile?" I supplied.

He shook his head. "More than that. It's— Uh-oh, here comes trouble."

The change in topic threw me; then my eyes tracked his gaze out to the parking lot.

Mr. V was exiting his car without his pugs in tow, and as he strode toward the door, I noticed the wariness in his eyes.

"What the hell?" Elijah remarked, but I had no time to explain because Mr. V swung the door open in a huff.

"Where is he?" he asked in an accusatory tone.

I stood my ground and folded my arms across my chest. "Dunno."

In my side view, I noticed Elijah's mouth drop open.

Mr. V pointed a finger at me. "You should've never—"

"I did what I felt was right," I replied in an even manner. "If you're going to cause trouble, I'll get the authorities involved."

That made Elijah spring into action. He straightened and reached toward the counter for his cell.

"No, I… You don't understand," Mr. V replied, his tone softer.

*It's not what you think. Michael…he's not hurting me…he's just…*

"I just need to know he's safe," he said in a conciliatory voice.

"I don't know anything," I responded. "I gave West a couch to sleep on, and by morning he was long gone."

"West?" V repeated, his head springing back. "Is that the name he's going by now?"

My eyebrows scrunched together. "What do you mean?"

"His name is Jonas. Jonas West Hollis. West is his…his mother's maiden…" He shook his head as if he shouldn't have been working through all that in front of me.

But I'd admit it was compelling. No wonder West looked so determined offering me that name last night. Jonas almost didn't sit right. But West certainly did.

V scratched his chin. "How did he even…?"

He let the question hang, but I didn't offer the part about him taking my bike. I wasn't sure why, except that if West needed to get away, he deserved that chance. He was a grown-ass man.

I straightened my shoulders. "I think it's a good idea you don't come back here anymore."

He nodded, pulled out his wallet, and fished out a business card. "If you hear anything, please let me know."

He made it seem so final, like West was gone for good.

And I almost felt sorry for him. *Almost.*

After he left, I told Elijah what'd happened the night before as I sipped my coffee and scratched Mack behind the ears.

"Holy fuck. You've got to be kidding me," Elijah remarked, placing his empty coffee cup in the basin and running the water to rinse it out. "He stole your bike?"

"*Borrowed*," I replied with a smirk. Maybe I was losing it. Guess I just gave the guy credit for doing whatever was needed.

"Suppose I'll have to visit your friend Kam's shop to buy a new one."

"Wait until Brin hears about this. Brooke too," Elijah said, finally brightening.

There was the Elijah I knew. He loved gossip, and this was definitely one hell of a crazy story.

# 3

# WEST

I LEFT MY ROOM AND WALKED TOWARD THE QUAD, WHERE THE showers were located. The hostel on W 25th Street was the cheapest place I could get at a moment's notice, and for now I'd be able to swing the daily rate until I got a better grip on my newfound existence. Quite honestly, I'd never felt so free in my entire life, even if I had to share a communal shower with six other people. I'd spent the better part of eight years grieving for everyone I loved, and though Michael had in his own way helped me through that and I'd forever be grateful for everything he'd provided me, it was time to move on.

I'd held on to any fragment of my past I could as it slipped through my grasp with each passing year, and Michael had become the only remaining shard. That, coupled with my guilt about wanting to break away after he offered me solace in his home, was what made me stay for so long.

The shower was free, so I shut the door behind me, twisted the knob, and walked under the warm spray. It wasn't fancy like Michael's shower with its jets shooting in different directions, but it felt like comfort and freedom. It reminded me that Michael and

I were never truly on equal footing, and that had niggled away at me for a long time.

Michael saw the world in black and white, the have and have nots, even knowing I had grown up poor. He wanted to give me everything, show me everything—everything superficial, that is—and though that intrigued me at first, deep down I knew it wasn't important. I would give up anything to have my family back, even if it meant living as poorly as before.

I did care for Michael in my own way, but the scales were unbalanced, and even though I told him I needed the space to figure some things out, he had too much pride to let me go. He was used to getting what he wanted, so my walking away left him feeling helpless and scared, not that he'd ever admit it. But I had to find a way out.

Which led me to thoughts of Tristan. I soaped my hair using the communal shampoo the hostel provided, and remembered how Tristan had offered me that out and how I'd taken it. I hadn't expected it to happen that night. I'd been carrying around a change of clothes and an envelope of cash for weeks. But that fight over me wanting to find a new job had sent me over the edge. *You'd be bottom of the barrel in a restaurant, and you're already on your way to being promoted at my firm.*

Somehow Tristan recognized I'd had enough. I appreciated that he didn't push me for any information, nor did he try to preach to me, which is what Michael did a ton. But I supposed he couldn't help it; he'd known me since I was a teen.

I shook away the thought that I've always found Tristan attractive, with his tall and thicker frame and soft blue eyes that seemed aware of everything. And the few times I'd gone in to pick up the pugs, I found myself shy in front of him. It wasn't that I didn't have any experience with men. Before Michael and I acted on our feelings, I had screwed around with plenty of guys. But something about Tristan was striking. His wavy brown hair with hints of chestnut, the scruff along his chin that I imagined would feel rough against my palm...

Tristan was probably around Michael's age, maybe older, but there was a different air to the man who owned the dog grooming business, along with a quiet confidence. A trace of sadness as well —one I'd recognized immediately in his eyes. I'd carried that same kind of melancholy like a torch into my twenties, and this was finally my opportunity to make a clean break, a fresh start.

I twisted the dial to turn off the shower, determined to make it on my own. First order of business was to find a job. If I was ever going to be able to afford a place to rent, even if it was with a roommate, I needed to make some cash. The amount I brought with me, that I'd saved from my previous job in Michael's investment firm, would only last so long.

After I toweled off in my room, I changed into the only nice pair of jeans and shirt I'd brought with me. My fingers reached for my hoodie, the one I wore almost as a defense mechanism, before I decided I was better off without it today. My plan was to tackle the row of restaurants down the street and get hired as a dishwasher or busboy. I smirked, thinking about how Michael would have a coronary if he knew I'd taken such a lowly position. *You shouldn't have to serve people. You're better than that.*

In his view, the service industry was beneath him, and I always hated how he treated people whose job it was to cater to his needs. Tristan noticed it too, I now realized. I'd observe their interaction through the car window sometimes and was secretly glad that Tristan never cowered in Michael's presence like others did.

According to the hostel desk manager, my best bet was to head to the bustling square near where Lorain intersected W 25th, which was considered the city's newest trendy area. If there was one thing Cleveland had, it was a plethora of restaurants. My goal was to work my way up to kitchen staff. I felt a pang in my gut thinking about my mom, who had taught me everything I knew about cooking. I clutched at the silver chain around my neck, which was a constant reminder of my roots.

*Maybe I'll make you proud, Momma.*

But she was long gone, they all were—it'd been eight years now, and thinking about them wouldn't do me any good. Most of the time I'd spent with Michael had been grieving for them. He'd helped me through so much just by being a solid presence, and I'd felt obligated to him. But I couldn't be anymore. People came into your life at the exact time you needed them to—that was on a greeting card I once saw.

A bunch of bullshit, but it was a nice thought.

As I headed down the stairs, one of the other tenants was climbing up. He was cute, and if I had to guess, a couple of years younger than me. We had both been in the common room last night, watching whatever channel the first person who'd arrived had turned on—those were the rules. Some crime detective show.

"You heading out?" he asked in a shy voice.

"Yeah, job applications," I replied.

"Well, good luck. Maybe I'll catch you later." I could tell he wanted me even last night, when he kept eyeing me over his water bottle. But I'd been too shaken, too freaked that I'd finally broken away from Michael's hold on me, and afterward had fallen into a fitful night of sleep.

I hadn't fucked anybody in a long time. Michael and I had merely been roommates the past few weeks because I'd pulled away from him physically as well as emotionally and he was grasping at straws to hold on. I was the one who'd started whatever had evolved between us the past couple of years, one night after we drank a bottle of wine and he was being sweet. He was kinder when he was tipsy, and I... I was horny and still finding my way.

I had made the first move; having resided in Michael's home for so long, I felt *comfortable* around him. I was grasping onto anything familiar at the time—and he was certainly all in after that—but it never felt right, not for me. I was so mixed up about it that I needed a chance to breathe. But he would never allow it. He was too damn intense all the time.

Michael had only been with one other man before he married Serena, and after they divorced, once we decided to become intimate, he'd fuck me into the mattress whenever the mood struck. Except, he was still pretty repressed, sometimes even pretending I was a family friend he'd taken in, which had all been true until that point.

And that was how I knew it was wrong—and time to leave. The guilt he felt about how our relationship had progressed sometimes mirrored mine, and it needed to end. The pugs were the only thing we seemed to bond over, anyway. I certainly missed Coco and Chloe, but the idea of them keeping him company helped relieve some of the burden. They slept on his side of the king-size bed, and only sometimes would Chloe gravitate toward mine. Maybe someday I'd have a dog of my own. But first things first.

After I climbed onto Tristan's bike, which I'd chained to the rack in front of the hostel with a lock I bought from the general store, I headed toward the square. I was grateful that Tristan had helped the idea click solidly in place in an offhand way by flipping to my favorite show on the Food Network the other night. Damn, I hoped he wasn't sore with me about his bike, not that it mattered—at this point, I'd never see him again.

I walked into Victor's restaurant as confidently as I could and came out with a job bussing tables. I started the day after tomorrow, and I had to give them the address of the hostel, which appeared to not register, let alone matter. Michael would liken the job to servitude—cleaning scraps off someone's table—but it was honest work, and I had to start somewhere. I was pissed at myself for allowing him to steer me away from my passion all this time. It wasn't about making money. Sure, it got you nice things, but they didn't sustain you.

After I stopped at a hot-dog stand at the corner nearest the restaurant, I rode to a Goodwill shop two blocks down to buy another pair of jeans and a couple of T-shirts. Thankfully, I'd be given a uniform of black pants and a white shirt from Victor's.

Christ, Michael would have a field day if he saw me now. Five dollars total spent on food and clothing, which wasn't a far cry from eight years ago when I showed up on his doorstep, penniless, with only the clothing on my back. Practically everything I'd ever owned had been secondhand until Michael came along. But then I heard my mom's voice in the back of my head. *There's no shame in living within your means, not when you're down on your luck.* My grandmother would add, *Someday it'll be your turn to shine.*

I wondered what they'd think of me swiping Tristan's bike to survive. My shoulders slumped. I'd have to come up with some way to return it or maybe pay him back. I wasn't one to accept handouts easily. I had even paid Michael for use of his things—rent, car, and utilities—from my modest paycheck as an office clerk. He didn't want to accept it, but I began placing the money in the desk drawer of his home office, and after a while he stopped mentioning it.

*Stubborn*, he'd say under his breath.

Later that night, I fucked that guy I ran into earlier on the stairs. I met him in the common area again, and he motioned with his head for me to follow him to his room. We didn't even ask each other's names.

It didn't matter; it just felt too good. Pure, raw sensation. Me, finally running the show—at least until we both got off.

I let him fuck me the following night, and after that I never saw him again, which was exactly how I wanted it. No ties, no obligations—except to myself.

## 4

# WEST

It'd been a month since I walked away from my life with Michael, and though there'd been moments of real floundering and maybe a bit of loneliness too, I was the happiest I'd been in years. Because I was simply me—bare and unfiltered. Just trying to survive and get back to who I really was before my life drastically changed nearly nine years ago.

I clocked out of Victor's after a long shift, collected my tips, and headed through the rear door toward Tristan's red bike. I was allowed to keep it chained to a post behind the restaurant next to the Dumpster, where some of the kitchen staff took their smoke break. I liked hanging around back there for a few extra minutes, hearing the dirt the cooks gossiped about. Like how one of the line chefs was always running late, making the sous chef lose his mind. There was a hierarchy in the kitchen, and you didn't want to cross those in charge, especially the head chef, who had the direct ear of the owner and manager. So I mostly kept my head down and did any work thrown my way.

Living at the hostel had become a costly daily expense, no matter how cheap the rate was. One day on my break, while scouring the classified section in the *Plain Dealer*, one of the servers I'd become friendly with asked if I was looking for a roommate. Marco had told me that he and his brother, Angelo, rented the first floor of a house in Ohio City, a neighborhood close to the restaurant, and they'd need a third occupant when their friend moved out at the end of that month.

The rent was cheaper than a month's stay at the hostel, plus Marco didn't ask many questions about why I was living there to begin with. I overheard enough to know they came from a family of immigrants, so they probably understood somebody down on their luck.

I was able to move in last weekend with little more than my backpack, my bike, and the clothes on my back. I had bought myself a few new pairs of jeans and shirts from the Goodwill store again, along with an older model cell phone with an affordable plan at a pop-up shop in the square, so for now I was set.

Besides, it wasn't like I had anybody to call. I had no living relatives—and the very thought of that sat like a stone in my gut—and any friends I had made as an adult were tied to Michael in some way, shape, or form. I'd even gotten my last job through his connections, and add that to the fact that everything in the high-end condo belonged to him, and it felt like nothing was ever purely mine. Until now. The worn jeans and the cast-off Chucks belonged to me, free and clear, and nothing made me giddier.

Once I got to my new apartment, which was about eight blocks away, I parked my bike in the garage and dug out my key. As I let myself inside the side entrance, I noticed how the blue paint was peeling on the small bungalow. The house was dated but cozy with its worn couches and flower wallpaper, and I counted myself lucky as I padded through the dark living room; my roommates were already asleep.

Had Marco been on evening shift tonight, he would've probably offered me a ride. I usually declined, though. Besides, I didn't want to be indebted to anyone, not even for a ride—not anymore.

It was well after midnight, and since I'd been allowed to work some swing shifts, I made better tips with the dinner crew than during the lunch crowd. Thus far, it'd been enough to pay for my rent and food for the month, and right now I was living on a week-by-week basis. No way could I afford wheels of my own anytime soon, but I didn't actually mind so much.

I was actually warier of the bike being stolen ever since I heard of some recent thefts in the area. That would bum me out, not only because it took away my sole form of transportation, but also because someday I wholly considered returning the bike to Tristan. Or buying it off him.

I actually felt guilty that I never properly thanked him.

As I crawled between the thinning sheets in the single bed, I thought about how someday I might thank Michael too. Maybe with time, he and I could speak like reasonable adults, with no hard feelings. I could explain that he had provided me a home when I was completely lost and broken. I could wish him well and tell him I hoped he found somebody to take care of the way he craved, but that I could never fall back into a similar situation with him or anybody else ever again. I had been vulnerable for far too long, and now I needed to get my life back.

On that hopeful note I fell asleep, but only for a few hours because my eyes still naturally blinked open around 5:45, the time Michael and I used to wake up. He'd work out in his home gym, and I'd shower and make coffee even though I wasn't much of a morning person. Then he'd drive us to work. He had completely absorbed me into his way of life, and I didn't even feel like myself the last couple of years.

Michael had a second vehicle I sometimes borrowed to attend college courses at CSU or run errands, except I always felt like a kid driving his parents' car. But it wasn't his fault; I had fallen right into the routine as well. Once I'd turned of age, I could've left. But truth be told, I was still adrift, struggling to overcome losing everything and everyone as a teenager. So I'd clung to Michael as some sort of safety net.

Even though I was only responsible for myself this morning, I still wrestled with getting back to sleep. I turned over and threw the comforter over my head, but nothing happened. I considered jacking off imagining the guy from my last hookup because his body was smoking, but I didn't think I had the energy, let alone the desire. Right then I wished I had Chloe's warm body next to mine, even if she snored worse than Coco.

I wondered if Tristan's dog—Mack, I think his name was—always slept with him, and how long Tristan had been single. Except I was assuming a lot. Was he even gay or bi? I expected so, but I didn't really know why. There'd been a couple of photographs in his apartment of himself with another guy. Guess I just supposed it was a past lover. Plus, that sadness in his eyes, like he was a guy who'd loved and lost.

Or maybe it was the way he'd look at me when I dropped off the dogs—a dude knew when another dude was checking him out—not that he was inappropriate in any way. Which was probably the only reason why I had followed him into his apartment that night. He felt safe, which was strange, since I didn't know him very well.

I suddenly remembered what time of morning it was and that Doggie Styles opened for business at six o'clock. When Michael wanted to get to the office early, he'd take the pugs in first thing when Doggie Styles opened. I rarely dropped Coco and Chloe off, but the times I did, Tristan was one of the staff who greeted me.

Before I could change my mind and reconsider what the hell I was doing, I was calling the grooming number affixed prominently on a magnet I used to see every time I reached inside the refrigerator at Michael's condo.

I held my breath, hoping it was Tristan who answered. Or not, so I could hang up immediately. Though I could do that now, and nobody would be the wiser.

"Doggie Styles." When I heard the voice on the other end, I recognized it straightaway.

It was Tristan, whose tone always sounded deep and friendly, but also a little hesitant, like maybe he was trying too hard to be cheerful.

My heart kicked up a notch. What in the hell was I doing?

Except I'd been hoping to thank him for that night.

"Your bike is sort of shitty, but it's helped me get around, and I'm, uh...totally grateful for that."

I heard a small gasp as he processed my words.

"I'm glad, *West*." I could hear the smile in his voice, and considered if it was because he was happy to hear from me too or if I amused him, which was exactly what I was trying to do to lighten the mood. Or maybe it was because he knew I was using a different name. I'd forgotten I was listed as the pugs' emergency contact as Jonas. Yep, I was totally thinking about this too hard. "Thanks for taking that crappy bike off my hands. I needed a new one anyway."

"You're welcome," I replied with a smirk, but then my hands started shaking, and I figured I'd said enough. "So, um, that was all I wanted to say."

I pushed the End Call button on my phone like it was an explosive.

Except I was unable to stop the grin from pulling at my lips as I rolled over on my stomach and replayed the exchange in my head. Totally relaxed, I fell into a deep sleep and dreamed of my family. My mom and grandma cooking Friday dinners for my siblings and me. We didn't have a lot of money, so it was normally cheap rice or pasta with whatever else was on sale that week. Unless it was the beginning of the month when Grandma's social security check would come in. One time we even had tenderloin with baked potatoes.

I'd sit on my favorite stool, chop some vegetables, and whip up some balsamic dressing for our salads, and I always imagined carrying on the tradition someday. But somewhere along the way, I had completely lost myself.

A few days later, I called Doggie Styles again. As soon as I began dialing the number, a sense of calm settled over me as if Tristan was some sort of lighthouse in the murky sea of my life. Which was ridiculous. But I did wonder if he had that effect on others. In fact, I found myself curious about a lot of things related to Tristan.

"Has Michael come looking for me?" I asked as soon as he answered.

Again, it took him a long moment to process my voice and my question. "*Yes.*"

My shoulders tensed even though it didn't surprise me. I could imagine Michael pacing and going ballistic, questioning where the hell I'd run off to. He was all-consuming and way too invested in my life, and that was the problem. My stomach throbbed in anticipation of my next question. "Is he...angry?" I shouldn't have asked, but now I couldn't take it back.

"Maybe," Tristan replied. "Seemed more concerned."

My shoulders unwound a fraction. Still, I sort of felt terrible for making him worry.

"How are Coco and Chloe? They doing okay?"

"I'm sure they are," he said, and I could tell he'd winced when he said it. "I told him not to come back. I...didn't want any trouble."

"He's not a bad guy." There I went defending him again. My guilt got the best of me every time. He was a grown man and could totally fend for himself. "I know what you're probably thinking."

He sighed. "I'm not thinking anything. I suppose I was just trying to help the situation. He thinks I'm in contact with you, and I had to set him straight. I didn't want him asking anymore. Thought you should be free to do your own thing, *West*."

"Yeah...yeah, I should." The way he said my name slinked

down my spine and felt too personal somehow. Not only that, but I found I liked it too much. "So, um...thanks. *Again.*"

*Fuck.* This was a terrible idea. Now I felt indebted to Tristan for sticking up for me. I pressed the End Call button on the phone and vowed never to call him again.

## 5

# TRISTAN

I PUSHED THROUGH THE GROOMING SIDE DOOR AT DOGGIE STYLES. It was a couple of minutes after six in the morning, and Brin had already opened the day-care end for us. I looked through the entryway and spotted Brin's dog, Tally, who followed him around in an adoring way. I had watched Brin grow into a mature young man in the space of a couple of years and find love.

Nick was great for him, and though I knew there was some sort of heartache there between them, Brin had come through big-time. I suspected the two of them would make a life for themselves, and it wouldn't surprise me if Nick moved into Brin's condo sometime in the near future.

"You good?" I called over to Brin.

"Yep," he replied around a yawn. "How about you?"

I nodded, petting Mack as he leaned against my legs. If I knew he'd go for it, I'd send him over to play with Tally, but she had all that puppy energy and was usually too much for him.

Brin suddenly appeared in the doorway, having finished setting out all the toys for the incoming canine customers. "Meant to ask—any more word on that situation with V and his ex?"

"Nah," I replied and then turned to make a pot of coffee at the side counter so he couldn't see my expression. It'd been almost six weeks since the incident with West, and I'd admit it was difficult to shake the guy from my brain. I didn't tell Brin that West continued to phone Doggie Styles around opening time every few days or that the conversations were always short. I had no idea why he called, except maybe I somehow represented his former life, and checking in gave him some sort of satisfaction.

He usually started his greeting by insulting my bike, which to anyone else's ears would've sounded like the bike was some vintage piece of trash that was steadily falling apart, instead of a gently used ten-speed. But each time I listened for his dig, I couldn't help grinning because I could also hear the gratitude behind the words. The bike was his sole form of transportation—I had gotten that much at least—something plenty of people took for granted, myself included.

Normally, he'd ask casual questions about my lineup of appointments for the day or whether I'd tuned in to the latest episode of *Chopped* on the Food Network, as if changing the channel the night he slept on my couch had somehow bound us together. But I also pondered if he simply needed to hear something normal from a familiar voice.

If I attempted to steer the conversation in his direction, he didn't give away much and usually hung up pretty quickly; the last two times he at least said goodbye properly. But I couldn't help questioning how he was really doing and if he needed anything. Except that wasn't what he wanted from me, that much was obvious, even if the rest of it wasn't. He seemed determined to make it on his own, and I thought that was admirable.

When the phone rang on the grooming side, I tensed. We didn't get many calls this early, thankfully. It gave us time to get enough coffee in our system while we set up for the day. I wondered if West would be on the other end of the line. I might've even hoped, though I wasn't exactly sure why.

"I've got it," I remarked to no one in particular since there was nobody on the grooming side except me. I rushed toward the handset before it stopped ringing. I nearly collided with the display we had set up for leashes and collars from one of our vendors. Christ, I was being ridiculous.

"Doggie Styles," I answered as calmly as possible.

I held my breath, which was absurd. You'd think I didn't have more important stuff going on in my life than a phone call every few days from a twenty-something guy who'd disappeared from one life to create another. Damn, when I thought of it in those terms, it sounded so surreptitious.

I could hear his disjointed breaths before he even spoke. They had a certain faltering rhythm when he was anxious. I noticed it that night in the car as well.

"The chain fell off your shitty bike," he said after what felt like an eternity.

I grinned. Couldn't help myself.

"Did you fix it?" I asked, and Brin gave me a strange look as he peered at me through the doorway. I waved him off and turned away from his watchful eye.

"Yeah, I can be pretty handy, actually," he replied. "If given the chance."

He muttered that last part, and it compelled me to ask, "What else?"

"What do you mean?" he asked, and I heard some rustling, which made me wonder if he was still in bed. The idea of him talking to me while beneath his sheets made me curious about so many damn things. Where was he? Why did he call me at six in the morning? Did he sleep in pajamas or in the nude? I immediately shook that thought away. Not going there.

"What other things...are you good at?"

I heard him inhale a sharp breath. "I... I'm not..."

"None of my business," I replied, giving him an out and hoping like hell he didn't hang up again. Why, I didn't quite understand yet. Maybe because he was safe, a distance away. There was no harm in talking to an interesting voice on the other end of a line. It'd been so long since I felt this kind of stirring curiosity about another person and their well-being. It was different than how I felt about my employees, who had become like a family, but I couldn't quite place my finger on why.

I'd admit there was some attraction there, but it was obvious neither of us needed that from the other, not that he was remotely interested in someone like me—older and sort of like a hermit, depending on who you asked around here.

So maybe we could become friends.

I'd actually like that. I couldn't deny that this guy intrigued me.

"Guess I was just curious since you're obviously interested in cooking," I remarked, remembering his keen interest in the show. "Though I suppose that doesn't make much sense since I watch those shows too and can barely boil a pot of water."

"Is that so?" he replied, and I could hear the grin in his voice.

"Yep. I have no idea why I watch, maybe just to pretend I'd learn by osmosis or something. But I tune in to the home network as well—those decorating shows are my favorite." Christ, I sounded ridiculous and definitely like a recluse.

"Decorating shows I can actually picture, considering your apartment seems pretty stylish...and orderly...and, uh, *spotless*," he said, his voice drifting as if visualizing it.

Now it was my turn to laugh. "Uh, yeah, I might have a little problem with cleanliness."

I noticed Brin making a face at me through the doorway, and then he laughed and rolled his eyes as if to say *understatement*.

"Nothing wrong with that," West replied in a lighter voice. "And you're right. I do enjoy cooking. Michael didn't exactly think it was a viable career—"

"Why the hell not?" I asked with a bit too much gusto, so I toned it down. "Plenty of people love to eat—me included."

"True." He snickered. "Michael turned his nose up at a fuckton of things. He saw himself as a pragmatist, but I just told him he was a snob."

*Don't I know it*, I wanted to say but instead only listened. He was finally being open about something, and thus far this was the longest he'd ever stayed on the phone.

"I always wished Michael would loosen up," he grumbled. "But the truth is, he took care of me, in his own way."

"I could see that," I replied. "Maybe a little too well sometimes?"

His laugh was humorless, and my stomach tightened. I hoped I hadn't said the wrong thing. So I remained silent until another sentence poured out of him.

"I lost everything, and his family took me in," West said in a far-off voice, like he was adrift in a memory. Damn. What in the hell did that mean? "I'll always be grateful."

"I... Damn. Thanks for sharing that. Obviously, I've wondered," I responded, though I had trouble knowing what to say. No way would I push him to clarify how he lost everything. "I can hear in your voice that you still care—"

"Not like *that*," he replied in a huff.

"That you're still *concerned*," I tried again, revising my statement. "He left me his business card, by the way. Do you want me to tell him you're okay? Unless you already did or were planning to—"

"No, I can't call him. He would... He'd only hound me about coming home, and I don't want to hear the guilt in his voice."

It was almost as if he were speaking of a parent rather than a past lover. So possibly there was a dynamic there I wasn't aware of, or maybe I had totally read their relationship wrong. The things he said about Michael being a caretaker certainly fit.

"Yeah, okay. I, uh... I wouldn't mind if you told him," he said suddenly as if making up his mind right then and there. "Thanks."

"Okay, I will." I could hear his breathing quicken, and I figured he was either going to change his mind or hang up. "Wait, before you hang up. In case you ever need anything outside business hours, here's my cell number."

He listened to me rattle it off before ending the call, and I had no idea if he wrote it down. It might've overwhelmed him, but I wanted him to have it regardless. Now that he actually shared more with me, I felt even more convinced that I was some sort of lifeline for him.

Brin was busy with a couple of customers on the day-care side, but he kept throwing me glances as I dug out V's card. Michael's card.

The number connected, and I heard Michael's imposing voice on the other end. "Hey, uh, Michael. This is Tristan from Doggie Styles. I thought you should know that West is okay. He called the shop to thank me for helping him out that night, and he wanted me to let you know he's fine."

"Where is he?" The immediate anger in his voice was like a lash against my ear. "What number did he call from?"

Christ, no wonder West wanted some space from the man.

I huffed out an exasperated breath. "Chill out—that attitude obviously didn't help you last time."

I could hear him panting into the phone and could almost imagine his nostrils flaring like some overbearing ape.

"I don't know where he called from," I finally responded. "Frankly, it's none of my business and no longer yours. Just passing on the message."

After I hung up, I pounded my fist into the counter. Damn, he was a sanctimonious bastard. Was he always that intense with West? Who knew where this protective instinct was coming from, but if West needed someone to help fend off a guy like Michael, I'd gladly step into the role.

6

# WEST

I CONTINUED CALLING TRISTAN IN THE MORNINGS AT DOGGIE Styles every few days. But I'd admit the late shifts were beginning to catch up to me. The manager had moved me into the kitchen a couple of nights a week, either as a dishwasher or a porter, which meant I was always scrubbing down one thing or another. But I didn't mind because it placed me in closer proximity to the chefs and the bustle of the kitchen, which was just as exciting and hectic as I thought it would be.

I couldn't place my finger on exactly why I kept contacting Tristan. Maybe he offered a soothing and rational voice on the days I doubted myself most. Now that I had his cell number, I considered phoning him in the evening instead, except I didn't dare cross that line. *Yet.*

But I did share a couple of additional things with him about my newfound life, namely that I was a busboy at a restaurant and that I found a place to live with a couple of roommates. Those details were ambiguous enough—he had no idea where in the city I worked or lived, and with under a million people in Cleveland, he could guess any dozens of neighborhoods east or west—

not that he would send out a search party for me. After all, he wasn't Michael.

I had to ask myself if I was only using Tristan as some sort of safety net, kind of what Michael had come to represent those first years in his home. But my feelings about Tristan were all kinds of mixed up. I actually found him wholly interesting, and I sort of wondered if we could be friends someday.

"Shit, he's late," one of the sous chefs remarked as I loaded the dirty dishes in the rack and pushed them through the automated machine. "One more time and I swear he's out."

I looked over at the line cook, who had placed a menagerie of vegetables on the counter for the prep cooks to begin chopping for the extensive menu.

I was pretty quiet at work outside of telling the line cook when the towels or dish soap were low, but this was one situation where I wanted to raise my voice and speak up. "If you need any help, I know how to dice onions and stuff."

A look passed between them as if considering it. The sous chef shook his head, and I turned away before they could see my deflated expression.

"You've done it before?" the line cook asked after the sous chef walked away.

The last time I'd prepped a meal was in Michael's kitchen for a dinner party when the chef he'd hired was suddenly short-staffed and I offered to help. Michael was irritated with me for doing work that was "beneath" me, but I couldn't help beaming all night.

"Only a couple of times, but I'm a fast learner," I said with as much confidence as I could muster. "I can do whatever you need."

"I need several vegetables prepped and chopped ahead of time for the daily specials. Let's see what you can do," he replied, and I felt giddy with excitement. Over chopping vegetables. Christ.

After I thoroughly washed my hands, I slipped on latex gloves. On the counter, the cook had placed carrots, onions, and celery to be diced and used as a base for the minestrone soup.

*If only Michael could see me now.* My thoughts drifted to my last conversation with Tristan a couple of mornings back.

"I called Michael like you asked," he'd said.

I felt instant relief, though I wasn't sure why. Was it because he did the hard work for me, or because I trusted him to help?

"Thank you," I replied.

"No problem. He, uh…sounded relieved but also angry."

I sighed. "That doesn't surprise me."

"I still didn't give him any information, not even about you borrowing my bike."

My heart pitter-pattered. "How come?"

"Dunno. To give you a fighting chance, I suppose. It's none of his damn business anyway. You're an adult."

Maybe that was why I continued to call him. It felt like he got me or something. And right now I needed people in my life I could trust. My roommates were cool and all, although I still didn't know if I had much in common with them outside of video games. Marco went cruising gay clubs a lot, and though I'd gone with him a couple of times, it was more important to pick up additional shifts at work when I could.

After dicing the vegetables, I helped the line cook prep bowls of lettuce and cucumbers at the salad station. Just as I was finishing up, the tardy prep cook arrived with an excuse about a flat tire, which his boss didn't seem to believe. And even though I had to return to washing dishes, I chalked it up to a good night.

I got home well after midnight, and after I washed up and stripped down to my boxer briefs, I lay in bed, thrumming with the need to tell somebody about my night. If my family were still alive, my grandmother would've more than likely stayed awake for me, because she suffered from insomnia and some nights she slept very little.

She'd have been in her favorite recliner beneath the lamp where she read her lifestyle magazines cover to cover. She would've smiled with joy for me, grabbed my face, and kissed my cheek. Tears suddenly pricked my eyes, and I turned over to rub my face against my pillow, the hole in my chest gaping.

I lifted my cell and flipped to the number I had stored in my phone. The one that Tristan had rattled off one morning. At the time, I figured I might need it in case of an emergency.

I used my thumbs to quickly type out the message before I deliberated too much about it. The worst that could happen was that he wouldn't respond. But then he'd also have my number, which could come back to bite me in the ass.

But I could trust Tristan, right?

**You awake?** I texted.

**Depends on who's asking me,** he replied after another minute.

Well, duh, he wouldn't know it was me. **This is West.**

There was a longer pause this time, so I speedily typed an additional comment.

**You said it was okay to use this number. But it might've been a stupid idea. Or too late. No worries.**

His response came promptly.

**It's not stupid at all. I'm here. What's up? Everything okay?**

I took a deep breath. Why was I messaging him in the first place? Well, it was too late now, and I couldn't not type something back after all he'd done for me. I chastised myself for that thought immediately. I still didn't owe him anything.

*Don't fall into the same trap.*

**Everything is pretty good actually. I was able to help the line cook in the kitchen today.**

**That's amazing. Tell me more. Call if you want.**

It would be easier to talk rather than type, and besides, I'd called him plenty of times at his job. Except, this was more personal since he was at home and likely in bed just like me. I took a deep breath and punched in the number before I chickened out.

He answered on the first ring. As soon as I heard his voice, my nerves instantly vanished.

"Do you always stay up late?" I asked. "Are you one of those people who don't sleep well?"

"Not usually. But Chris used to have that problem, and sometimes his tossing and turning would keep me up," he said, and for some reason my stomach dipped in anticipation. But before I could get another thought out, he added, "Chris was my husband. I lost him almost three years ago. We'd known each other since we were eighteen, so it's sort of a hard habit to break."

"Fuck, I'm sorry." I realized that I didn't know much of anything about Tristan, and now I wanted to. We all have a history, after all. Suddenly I remembered noticing the dulled silver band he wore on his ring finger as he gripped the steering wheel that night.

"No, it's okay. It's definitely been a hard adjustment." He took a deep breath and shifted on his mattress. At least that was what it sounded like. "But I'm good. In fact, his family is coming over tomorrow for lunch."

I sat up a little. "You still have a relationship with his family?"

"Yeah, like I said, we've known each other for almost twenty years. I don't have a family of my own, so..."

*Neither do I*, I wanted to say; it was on the tip of my tongue. Not many people knew except Michael, but it felt safe telling Tristan. Besides, he was once removed through the phone line.

"Everyone has a family," I replied instead. "You came from somewhere."

"Okay, sure. I was in foster homes my entire life, so...the biggest thing I ever took away from that miserable experience were the pets—hamsters and cats and mostly dogs. Animals are loyal."

"Damn, that sucks," I replied. "Though I suppose it makes a ton of sense."

"Why, because I own a grooming business?" He chuckled, and the mood instantly lightened.

We talked for almost another hour about how Chris had encouraged him to start the business, and then about my job at the restaurant, until we both yawned one too many times. I realized I liked hearing the sound of his voice, so I kept asking him questions until eventually the conversation turned back to Chris. His tone changed to one of sadness and nostalgia as he explained how they bought a condo on the lake because Chris loved sunsets.

"We got married on a trip to Key West about ten years ago, and even though at the time it wasn't legally binding, it didn't matter."

"That why you still wear your wedding band?" I asked, and he became quiet. Fuck, I had put my foot in my mouth. But maybe he was only surprised I'd noticed.

"Yeah," he murmured. "Comforts me, helps me remember."

"I understand." It must've been so difficult to lose him. It was right on the tip of my tongue to tell him about missing my own family, about wearing my own memento of them, but I just couldn't find the right words, so I bid him good night instead.

"Night, West," he said in a sleepy, sexy voice that sent gooseflesh along my arms and legs. "Thanks for calling."

As I hung up, I was already thinking about the next time I'd phone him, and I cursed myself for looking forward to it.

*Friends are important*, my mom would say, even before I came out to her. *But make sure they like you for you. Don't let them change you. You're too special.*

I shut my eyes and let the tears flow.

7

# TRISTAN

I WOKE UP GROGGY FROM STAYING UP SO LATE ON THE CALL with West.

But it seemed like he needed to talk, needed someone to share his news with. He'd sounded so excited about being able to chop vegetables in the restaurant's kitchen. Just the simple joy of feeling useful doing a task you enjoyed. And instead of pulling teeth to get words out of him, he was more forthcoming with the conversation, even though I did most of the talking. But it'd been forever since I stayed on the phone that long with anybody, and besides, it'd been worth it getting to know West better.

I didn't want to put too much stock into it, in case he decided to bail, which was still likely given his state of mind the last few weeks. The best thing I could do for West was just be a sounding board, a safe person to call if he needed anything.

I took Mack for a walk down Lake Avenue, where he waddled along and sniffed at every patch of grass; then I came back home to prep things for lunch with Chris's family. I loved them dearly, but there was so much pain that remained between us. Still, it was a comfort to have somebody in my life who got what I was going through, albeit in a different way.

Later in the afternoon, I had invited my employees for some pool time at the condo. I considered them family too, so all in all, my life was pretty full. Except for the lonely spot in my soul that nothing ever seemed to fill. Not since Chris left the world.

"Hey there," I said, opening the door for Chris's mom, Judy, and his sister, Sheri. We hugged and kissed cheeks, and as we walked to the concrete balcony overlooking the lake, I noticed how his mom lingered on the photo of Chris that I kept on the end table. Losing a lover was one thing; losing a child had to be brutal, and I saw the aftereffects in her eyes.

As we settled onto the wicker furniture and caught up on our lives, I served them chicken salad on croissants I bought from my local deli, which offered specialty foods, including Chris's mom's favorite sea-salt-chocolate-chip cookies.

"Have you considered taking the boat out?" Judy asked as her gaze swept over the lake, which was as clear and flat as glass today. It was perfect sailing weather.

Chris and I owned a boat that was docked about ten minutes away at Whiskey Island, but I just couldn't bring myself to go there. Not yet. It was a huge responsibility, and we'd always taken it on together. Chris wasn't a fan of sailing, so he only did it for me, and though I enjoyed being on the water, it became burdensome when he was diagnosed with a malignant brain tumor almost four years ago. Despite the chemo and radiation, he only survived a year before he succumbed to his illness.

"I..." I shook my head. "You guys are welcome to use it."

"You can always sell it," Sheri suggested.

"I can," I admitted. But the notion didn't sit well with me, either.

"Maybe see what shape it's in?" Sheri proposed. "If you need me to go with you, I absolutely would."

"Good idea." The thought of it didn't seem quite as overwhelming anymore. "Maybe I'll even head there this weekend."

We talked and ate and laughed for the next couple of hours.

As I showed them to the door, I thought about how much I owed them, though they'd never see it that way. They'd only tell me that family stuck by each other in dark times. They suffered the same heartache as me, and though I learned to live with the pain, I especially missed having Chris around in my day-to-day life. We had been a team, and it was tough to go it alone after so many years.

For some reason, my thoughts drifted back to West. He was trying to make it on his own as well—we had that in common at least.

Later that afternoon, my employees showed up with their significant others to hang out by the pool. Brooke and her husband had brought the kids, and they were having a blast splashing each other in the water. Brin and Nick sat in lawn chairs with their hands linked, looking totally sweet together. Elijah seemed distant, and Stewart appeared frustrated about something, so I couldn't exactly place my finger on what was going on with the two of them. Except it certainly seemed they were more unhappy than happy lately.

As Nick slathered lotion on Brin's shoulders, I felt an ache deep in my chest. I missed Chris like crazy. I spun my wedding band around my finger, hoping he was out there somewhere, listening.

*I'll be with you forever. Just talk to me if you need me.*

*I'll always need you*, I'd replied through a flood of tears. Some days they never stopped flowing, and I felt like I would float away on a sea of my own sorrow.

I shifted my gaze to the blinding sun, feeling a calm settle over me.

*Maybe you are out there somewhere.*

My thoughts soon wandered to West, and I imagined him showing up to hang out with this group. I wasn't sure if I could picture it or not. Maybe because it'd been so long since I'd actually laid eyes on him, he almost seemed like a figment of my imagination.

Later that evening I found myself thinking about West again as I lay in bed. He hadn't texted or called, which was probably for the best. I didn't want to rely on his companionship, and besides, it'd been a busy day and I was totally exhausted, which helped me drift off to sleep more easily.

It wasn't until the following night that my cell buzzed with a text, and I felt almost relieved.

**So how long have you had this shitty bike?**

I smiled because the bike had become our link and it always seemed to come back to that.

**Maybe six years. Bought it secondhand. Thought I'd use it more frequently. Chris said he'd buy one too but never did. I only rode it sparingly.**

**See, you needed someone to take it off your hands.**

**LOL.**

When the phone rang suddenly with his number flashing on the screen, my pulse kicked up.

"How was your lunch with Chris's family?" he asked rather seamlessly, as if we'd been talking on the phone for hours. I liked that he was feeling more comfortable. But it wasn't face-to-face, and I certainly had no idea where he was calling from, which only lent to the mystery surrounding him.

I'd admit the fact that he'd called Chris by name made my stomach tilt uncomfortably, if only because it sounded so intimate. And more final.

"They're my family too," I replied a little too urgently. Maybe because I never wanted to lose sight of that fact. "It was good. They actually made me think about our boat."

"You own a boat?" he asked with an air of awe in his voice.

"It's not huge—just a twenty-seven-footer we bought off a friend. It doesn't do well in big swells, but watching the fireworks and the air show from the deck is spectacular."

"Whoa, that *would* be awesome," he replied.

This year I'd watched the downtown pyrotechnics from my apartment balcony, alone, not feeling like entertaining anybody this Independence Day or the ones before either.

"So, you're cool being out on the water?" I asked more tentatively, still nervous I was prying too much. "Some people aren't. Chris didn't love being on the lake all that much. Neither does Mack." I chuckled to myself at the memory of Chris carrying our reluctant dog back to the car, relief evident in his eyes that Mack had given him an out. "But for me, there's just something serene and primal about being on a wide expanse of water, where you see blue every direction you look."

"I actually never learned how to swim," he said in a quiet voice. "And Michael sort of had a water phobia, so we never went near Lake Erie."

*Michael.* Was that sadness I detected in his voice? Was he having a hard night?

"Dunno how long you and Michael were together, but it'll get easier being on your own. It was brave what you did," I said around a scratchy throat, hoping like hell I hadn't overstepped any bounds. "Just wanted you to know that. Lots of things take courage. Loss is hard."

"Don't I know it," he mumbled, and I was surprised by his response. One, because he wasn't angry with me for bringing up the situation; and two, because he seemed to be referring to something else, something deeper, more personal.

"Yeah?" I asked, hoping he'd continue but not wanting to push too much.

He didn't speak for several long seconds as if working up the nerve.

"Thing is, I…lost my entire family. In a house fire," he explained, and I reached for my sheets and fisted them tight. Something caught in my throat like thick syrup. "My mom, grandma, and two sisters."

A sharp gasp escaped me before I could tamp it down.

"Michael's wife, Serena, was a distant relative through marriage, and she agreed to take me in. Social services allowed it because there was a familial connection. She wasn't any kind of replacement, though. In fact, she paid me no attention," he muttered. "And Michael was always at work."

"Goddamn, West. I'm so sorry," I replied, even though it seemed insufficient for something so heartbreaking. "How old were you?"

"Sixteen. After I graduated high school, Serena left him, and...Michael said it was cool to stay. He helped me sign up for college courses, and after working in fast food for a few months, he got me an entry-level job with his company," he expounded. "We were quite a pair. He was hurting from his divorce, and I was only a shadow of myself. He sort of stepped up as a support after she was gone, helped me get through my days by adding structure to my life, and because I was so lost, it felt like a comfort back then."

My heart was beating out of my chest. Holy fuck. What exactly was the nature of their relationship? Had I read it all wrong?

"I know what you're probably thinking," he said, as if reading my thoughts. "But it wasn't like that. Michael and I had become more roommates than anything else. At least at first."

I took a deep breath and waited him out while my brain spun through the possibilities.

"When I'd hook up with guys and stuff, I could tell he was uncomfortable, and I didn't really know why at that time. I thought maybe he was homophobic"—he explained—"until one night when he looked at me a certain way. That's when I knew he was into men too. Later, I learned he had been with one other guy in his life."

My mind was reeling trying to fit the pieces together. How

long ago had that been, I wondered. I clenched my fist, hoping like hell he'd continue explaining.

"I'm the one who made the first move a couple of years ago. I was still so mixed up at the time," he said around a strained voice, and my heart went out to him. "Still lonely and sad and...lost, I guess."

"Yeah, *fuck*. I bet. That explains why it seemed so muddled between the two of you." I waited a beat and then said, "Michael definitely has feelings for you."

"In his own way, he does." He let out a heavy breath. "*Fuck*... I don't know why I'm telling you all of this."

"Because somehow it's safer to say the shit inside your brain over the phone?"

"Is that why you told me stuff about your relationship?"

"Yeah, maybe. I haven't reminisced about Chris in a while, at least not outside my own head," I admitted. "Plus, you're easy to talk to."

"Yeah...you too," he said, and my chest squeezed tight. "Though I don't really know what I'm doing; why I keep... I really should stop contacting you."

"Your choice," I replied in a steady voice even though my heart was beating like a drum. "Except, what harm is it doing?"

"I'm just... I'm supposed to be looking out for myself," he huffed. "Figuring my life out on my own. Not calling you and—"

"It's human to want a connection with somebody," I replied before he had the chance to discount it. "That's what this is. And...I look forward to it too."

I heard a little catch in his throat before he sputtered. "I... can't... I should go."

The phone call ended, and I lay staring at the ceiling for a long time, wishing I hadn't uttered that last part. But I was nothing if not upfront. I wasn't going to play games, not at my age, and not with a guy who was hurting a whole hell of a lot too.

I absently twisted my wedding band around my finger,

hoping this wasn't the end of our communication, but if it was, I was grateful for the past couple of months. In his own way, West had given me something different to focus on. As well as reflect on. I needed to start doing things I loved again or at least put old ghosts to rest so they didn't eat away at me any longer.

# 8

# WEST

It was early Sunday morning, and I was lying on the floor with a controller in my hand, trying to beat my roommates at *Mario Kart*. My thoughts naturally drifted to Tristan, wondering if he even owned a gaming system. Michael mainly used our Xbox to watch DVDs. He'd never dream of spending hours playing mindless games—he'd rather bring home extra work and stay in his home office all day long.

Why had I shared so much with Tristan our last phone call? It'd left me feeling open and vulnerable. And something else I couldn't quite put my finger on, especially when he admitted he looked forward to our calls as well.

Except, he was just a voice on the phone, and that was a tenuous connection at best. I didn't have to call, he didn't have to answer. He didn't know where I lived or worked. He couldn't control me or harm me. He didn't even try to use the number—he always waited for me to contact him first. So why was he starting to feel like so much more? Like a real friend. Like someone I could trust.

I told him my family had died in a fire—information even my

roommates and coworkers didn't know. Fact was, my family had rented a neglected house in a run-down part of town; in hindsight, the house should have been considered a fire hazard. I had been out that night at a high-school football game and had returned to my neighbors standing on the lawn, my house already engulfed in flames. They were all gone—just like that, in the blink of an eye.

A shiver raced across my shoulders at the thought of them struggling to breathe. *Survivor's guilt.* The therapist the county had assigned me had called it that.

What if I'd been home and able to save them? What if I had also perished? At least we'd all be together. If you bought into any of that shit. But the thought was a constant comfort to me—that at least they had each other. My fingers found the silver chain around my neck. My mom and grandma believed in the afterlife, and even in my desperate hours, they would've told me to keep the faith.

But here I was, alone, with barely two nickels to rub together, and everything in my life had changed yet again; except in a lot of ways, I was more myself than ever before.

I heard my cell ping with a text. It was near my thigh on the carpet. *Tristan.*

It was the first time he'd reached out to me using this number.

**If you're free today, I'll be down at Whiskey Island Marina, Slip 23, fixing up my boat. Might even take her out for a spin. No pressure.**

Immobilized, I stared down at the message, my heart thumping in my chest. But I just couldn't get my fingers unstuck from the controller, even though I'd already crashed long before the finish line in the game.

A longing surged inside me at the invite. Mixed with warring emotions. I wanted to go, and no fucking way did I want to go.

*It's just a boat ride.*

*But it's an in-person boat ride.*

*What the hell else do you have going on?*

I pushed my cell away from me on the rug, ignoring the pull I felt as we started a new round on the console.

"What do you guys have going on today?" Marco asked. "My shift starts at five. You're off today, West?"

I nodded. Sundays had become one of my days off, along with Wednesdays, even though I picked up additional shifts for extra money whenever I could. I didn't want to share an apartment with two guys and use a bike for transportation the rest of my life. Besides, culinary school would cost money too if I decided to go that route. I had only ever taken a couple of community classes, rationalizing to Michael that I wanted to learn how to cook for him. When he worked late or went away on business, I'd make all kinds of concoctions and then eat the evidence.

Thinking back on it made me ball my fist, the fact that his influence had run so deep. That I had to somehow live up to his standards just because he had opened his home to me. And now that I was free of him—of anyone—I was finally able to ask myself what I truly wanted.

"I got a hot date," Angelo said, steering his car away from the ditch on the screen.

"Yeah?" Marco asked, wiggling his eyebrows. "Same girl you saw last week?"

He nodded and made the hand motion to indicate an hourglass figure, and I had to laugh. Guys always had sex on the brain whether they were straight or gay. Well, most at least. I wasn't sure about someone like Tristan. But damn if he didn't do it for me when I allowed my brain to go there in my fantasies at night. I imagined ruffling his perfectly rational demeanor, making his calm, soothing voice get all rough and throaty as I took him from behind, or whatever else my ridiculous mind conjured up.

"How about you?" Angelo asked, shaking me from my thoughts.

"Nah." I shrugged. "I'm just out of a relationship, remember?"

He smirked. "Nothing wrong with hooking up or just having fun."

*A boat ride would be fun.*

I'd had several hookups these past couple of months, but they didn't satiate that hollow place inside me that'd been empty for too long. Something even Michael couldn't fill. Besides, he was pretty hands-off after sex, which was usually quick and always felt one-sided. Sometimes I just wanted him to hold me, but asking him felt all wrong, especially when he'd roll out of bed like he was on fire.

Truth was, I missed simple human contact. But that was awkward to ask for with a hookup, unless they were looking for the same thing. Maybe it wouldn't be such a strange request on Grindr or Tinder. My cheeks colored. Yeah, it probably was.

Regardless, I was being rude to Tristan by not responding to him.

After I crashed and burned in the game, I picked up my phone and texted him back. **Probably not. Got stuff to do around here.**

I held my breath, waiting for his response.

**No worries. Have a good day.**

Somehow that didn't sit well with me either.

After the game, I took a shower and got dressed, my eyes flashing to my hoodie hanging on the doorknob. I hadn't worn it in weeks, not since I walked away from Michael. I realized that it had somehow become a form of armor, a way to hide. Michael despised it, but I wore it anyway almost as a method of protest. Besides, it was one of the only things I had left from my adolescent self. I had arrived at his house as a sixteen-year-old wearing it, and because of that he knew he had no say.

After I walked to the grocery store with Marco, I listened to some music to relax, but my body was thrumming with too much pent-up energy. I slipped into my shoes and stepped outside to Tristan's bike, the shiny red metal gleaming in the sun. My pulse was pounding, and I hadn't even left the driveway yet.

*What if seeing him crosses some imaginary line?*

*What if he wants his bike back?*

I smirked to myself.

*He wouldn't do that to you.*

With that thought clicking solidly in place, I began riding toward the Shoreway, where the boat docks were located.

Once I crossed over to Edgewater Park and rode past the beach entrance, there was no turning back.

When I got to the docks I hopped off my bike, headed toward the slips, and searched for number 23.

As soon as I spotted Tristan, my feet faltered.

He was wearing cutoff khaki shorts and a worn blue T-shirt that matched his eyes. He was holding a large sponge he'd just dipped in a bucket sitting on the bottom of the boat. The sunlight reflected the auburn in his unruly hair.

I forced my eyes away from Tristan's tall frame and lean physique, and let my gaze rove over his boat. It wasn't new, but it didn't look beat-up either. It was large enough to hold a few friends, but not too huge or flashy. The brand Sylvan was brandished on the side along with some serial numbers. Michael would snub his nose at such a purchase, only wanting the best so he could show it off to friends and clients. Tristan didn't seem to share any of those qualities.

It struck me right then how attractive Tristan was. Not only his looks, but his level head and quiet confidence.

It brought me peace somehow. To know there was somebody in my corner. If he didn't want anything to do with me, we wouldn't have spent so many hours talking on the phone.

Unless he wanted something from me. If that were the case, wouldn't he have asked to see me sooner?

My pulse thundered in my ears as I considered turning around and heading back home. Instead, my feet felt like they were stuck in cement as I stood there and gawked.

## 9

# TRISTAN

I SCRUBBED HARDER AT THE SIDE OF THE BOAT EVEN THOUGH THAT section was already clean, angry at myself for even asking West to come out here today. What'd come over me?

He didn't want to be buddies in real life. So we talked on the phone a few times; big whoop. He was just looking for someone to connect with, was probably just lonely—and fuck, who wouldn't be after that tragic story—and because I was too, I had to go and open my big fat mouth.

When I heard some seagulls squawking on the deck, I glanced over my shoulder, and my breath caught in my throat.

West stood beside my bike, with his lip fished between his teeth, as if wholly unsure of himself; he was like a breath of fresh air.

A full head of dark hair, warm eyes, thick eyelashes, shorts, and a T-shirt. No hoodie. Damn, he was adorable.

He walked unsteadily toward the boat. "How's it going?"

I smiled. "You made it."

"Yeah, I wasn't sure, so..." He shrugged. "Didn't want to get your *hopes* up or anything."

I barked out a laugh. I actually enjoyed his sense of humor.

"You might've," I replied, and there was honesty in my statement. "It's not as much fun on the water alone."

His gaze darted the length of the boat, and for some reason it was like he was inspecting *me*, which was totally absurd. Thankfully, there wasn't much to clean besides cobwebs; it'd been in storage since Chris's diagnosis. She even had half a tank of gas, so I'd fired her up earlier and let her run for a few minutes. Luckily, she still purred.

It was ridiculous how much I'd missed this.

"Looks like the bike is still holding up well," I said, motioning to the fiery red ten-speed.

He bit the inside of his cheek, as if embarrassed that he was showing up with a stolen bike. But then I saw a momentary frisson of fear dart through his eyes, as if I'd actually reclaim his only mode of transportation. I knew he relied on that bike on a daily basis, so that moment of vulnerability from him only endeared him to me more.

"It's yours free and clear, okay?" I said, and when he let out a breath, I knew I had read him well. "No need to give it another thought."

"I always figured I'd pay you back," he began, but I didn't let him finish.

"Don't even think about it," I replied, waving my hand.

"No, I want to," he replied in a more forceful voice. "I don't want to be indeb—" He cut himself off and shook his head as if regretting his choice of words.

He was going to use the word *indebted*, and he was referring to his history with Michael; I discerned that much at least. I also knew how much he needed to have his independence.

"You know what? Sure," I conceded. "We'll figure out a way for you to pay me back."

When our eyes met and held, he nodded once.

"How about you chain your bike to that post and then come

on the boat? I'll show you around," I said. "Unless you changed your mind, which is fine."

He shook his head and dragged his bike toward the wooden post, securing the chain around the tire. I squatted down, squeezed the sponge out in the pail, and then wiped my wet hands on my shorts. West looked along the perimeter of the boat as if not sure where to step.

I stood up, walked over to the hull on the starboard side, and held out my hand. His eyes met mine briefly before he took it, and I helped pull him onto the deck.

His hand was smaller than mine and warm. As soon as he got inside, he dropped our linked fingers and looked away, color rising on his cheeks. "So, you've been cleaning all morning?"

"Yeah," I replied. "There were cobwebs, and I needed to check to make sure the motor still worked okay."

I wouldn't tell him how I found one of Chris's old swimsuits jammed in the corner of the cabin and had myself a good cry. He didn't need to hear my sob story. He had one of his own, after all.

His eyes darted to the stern, where the outboard motor was located. I expected the usual question about why the motor was located in the back of the boat instead of near the bow, but it didn't come. "And does it?"

"Yep, was just getting ready to fire it up again and go for a ride along the breakwall." I motioned toward the large body of water we lived on. "Feel like tagging along?"

His shoulders tensed up, and he stared out at the shoreline. I wasn't sure if he was nervous about the water or about being trapped alone on a boat with me. I didn't know if he still considered me a stranger, but after all our phone calls, it no longer felt weird to me. Sure, maybe to not have to *imagine* his reactions or what he looked like when he was right in front of my eyes, but that was about the only difference so far.

"The waves are low today, so no worries about the boat rocking, if that's a concern," I said, remembering what Chris always told me he was fearful of. "You can even wear a life vest."

"Nah, no vest, but..." He looked around the boat, scanning for something. "At least just tell me where they're located?"

"Of course." I patted one of the long red vinyl-covered seats. "They're under here."

I opened the portal and yanked one partially out to show him. They were made of bright orange floatation material that was coast-guard approved, and we even kept a couple of kids' sizes for friends with families. "All set, then?"

As soon as he nodded, I set to work before he changed his mind. It would be nice having company out on the water.

After I fired up the engine and let it run for a couple of minutes, I explained how to untie the ropes from the cleats on the dock on both the port and bow sides.

"I just need you to help me push off," I yelled over the motor. I motioned with my hand that he was to give the dock a good shove so the boat could propel backward.

He did exactly as I'd demonstrated, so I was able to back out of the slip, and once he got his footing and sat down on a seat near the stern, we began motoring toward the breakwall. Wake wasn't permitted until we were past the miles-long stone structure, so it was a smooth and calm ride to begin our small excursion.

We passed a couple of boaters, who waved in our direction.

"Is that a thing?" he asked, lifting his hand in a wave, as if it came automatically to him. Damn, he was cute.

"Guess so," I replied with a smirk. "There are definitely boater rules and such."

He sat back in the seat and shifted to get comfortable as he looked along the docks, which were lined with boats of all sizes, and I realized that my sour morning was turning into a very nice day.

# 10

# TRISTAN

Once we got past the breakwall, I revved the engine and sped up just a tad to feel that freedom I always did when I got out on the open water. And by this point, I asked myself why I'd waited three years to come out here again. But I supposed it just didn't feel right all those months until this very moment.

"You okay?" I asked West over my shoulder.

He nodded with a smile as he pushed the hair whipping in his face out of his eyes. "You gonna go any faster?"

I grinned in his direction. He had a little daredevil in him. Guess I shouldn't have been surprised. He'd "*borrowed*" my bike in the dead of night after all.

"Hang on," I shouted and then gunned the engine.

Before we knew it, we had jetted quite a distance on the open water, and I heard him shout as he raised his fist. "Holy fuck, is this exhilarating."

It was definitely thrilling and cathartic, at least for me. Chris would only ever indulge me for a few minutes before he asked to return to normal speed. I'd always try to pretend to ignore his first request until he'd ask again and call me a brat, and then I'd push the throttle to slow it down for him so we could cruise at a more leisurely pace.

We cruised all the way to the shallow inlet by the Rock and Roll Hall of Fame and the Science Museum on the W 9th Street pier, where slowing down to a reasonable speed was required again.

"It's so cool to see all this from the water," he said, marveling at the landmarks this city had to offer. He stood up to move toward the captain's chair and held on to the side rail as we drifted past the art-deco building. "I've only ever been inside once during an Elvis Presley exhibit. The man had a fondness for jumpsuits."

I laughed as we coasted past the Science Museum and turned west toward the football stadium that sat empty nearby but would soon be gearing up for opening weekend.

"You a fan?" I asked, glancing at him in my side view.

"Of the Browns?"

I nodded.

"More than I'm willing to admit," he replied, and I found myself smiling. "My grandmother was a die-hard."

I saw the brief sadness filter through his eyes before they cleared.

We talked preseason picks for a few minutes, and I was pleasantly surprised to find another sports fan in the fray. Chris watched all kinds of sports, but he definitely loved the Cavs and his beloved basketball teams most.

Once past the stadium, I sped up a bit, throwing West off balance and forcing him to take the seat across from me where the life vests were located. I doubled back toward Edgewater Beach, which was crowded with sunbathers and swimmers alike, and the closer to the shoreline we got, the splotches turned into shapes. I stayed a distance away from the beach and cut the engine.

The sun was beating down, and I was still drenched from

having worked on the boat all morning. Damn, I hoped I didn't smell too sweaty. Without another thought, I ripped my shirt over my shoulders and balled it up in order to wipe the perspiration from my forehead and the back of my neck. I could feel West's eyes on me, but I didn't turn in his direction, nervous about what I'd find in his gaze. Neither disgust nor admiration would sit well with me—I wouldn't know what to do with either option.

"I'm going to drop anchor for a little while," I said, finally meeting his scrutiny head-on. His cheeks were flushed, either from the sun or the heat. Or maybe from my bare chest—I hoped I wasn't making him feel uncomfortable. Christ, I was thinking way too hard about this. "If you're cool with that. You don't get seasick, do you?"

"I guess I wouldn't know. But I don't think so," he said as his eyes traveled over my torso before quickly turning toward the beach. We were close enough to make out some people in the water. "Why do you ask?"

I held up a finger as I stepped to the bow of the boat, opened the storage portal, pulled out the anchor, and threw it over the side. I watched it go down before backtracking to the captain's chair and thrusting the boat in reverse, hoping to apply tension to the rode so the anchor would affix to the bottom of the lake. "Some people—Chris, for example—wouldn't be able to do this for very long. The slow motion of the waves hitting the sides made him want to hurl."

I remembered the first time it happened. He held on to his stomach, pitched forward, and threw up off the side of the boat.

"Good to know," he said, shucking his own shirt. As he spread out on the long seat, he sighed, tilting his head to the sun, and I tried not to stare too long at his lean chest, his smooth brown nipples, and the fine line of dark hair that disappeared behind his waistband. He wore a delicate silver chain, but I couldn't exactly tell what was hanging from it except that it was thin and round. Soft brown freckles dotted his shoulders and matched the scattered ones on his cheeks. I didn't want him to feel on display, so I bent to reach for the sunscreen beneath the captain's chair.

"So far it only makes me want to nap," West murmured as I slathered the lotion on my arms and neck.

"Same," I replied, and I noticed how his gaze was focused on watching me smooth the sunscreen over my upper chest, which had patches of chestnut-brown hair near the center, whereas his was smooth shoulder to shoulder. I wasn't packing muscle either, but I had weight on him even though I'd kept myself trim over the past few years. Grief would do that to you.

"Here," I said, handing him the bottle. "The sun could be brutal out here. You'll want to use this."

He nodded and fished it from my fingers as I looked out at the horizon, making sure we were in a good spot and that I didn't see any motorboats coming too close.

"Uh, would you...*mind*," he asked, and when I turned, his fingers patted the back of his shoulder. "I burn really easily."

I already had a base tan from lying out by my pool at the condo, but his smooth fair skin was lightly pigmented everywhere, even on his legs.

My fingers worked fast over his shoulders and down to the small of his back because I didn't want him to think I was ogling him, even though I was trying hard to control my runaway breaths.

"There you go," I said, in a shallow pant. "Now you'll smell like coconut instead of rosemary."

A blush crawled along his cheeks as his breath hitched. I hadn't meant to say that out loud. Fuck. "It's just... That night you were at my place, I thought you..." I shook my head. "But maybe it was your shampoo or something. Just ignore me."

I placed the lotion within easy reach in the side storage pouch near the steering column, wishing the lake would swallow me up.

"How about basil?" West remarked, and when I looked over at

him, his lips wore a charming smirk. "I had to chop a bunch of that the other day."

He was letting me off the hook, and damn, I could've kissed him for that.

"You're going to make my stomach growl," I said, and he smiled. "I love Italian food. Well, any food really."

"Yeah? Do you have a favorite dish?" he asked as I sat down on the cushion across from him and lay back to soak in the sun.

"Not really. I'll pretty much eat anything you put in front of me," I said. "As I mentioned, my skills in the kitchen are lacking."

"I guess I come by it naturally. My mom and grandma were excellent cooks." His voice wavered on that last word before he recovered. I noticed how his fingers skated across his necklace, fingering what looked to be a silver ring.

When he noticed me looking, his eyes suddenly drifted to my hands, as if trying to spot my wedding band, and that helped me put two and two together. "Did that belong to your mother?" I asked in a gentle voice, not wanting to dredge up any sad memories.

"Yep." His fingers latched on, tugging the chain away from his body to show me. "It's called a mother's ring. Each stone represents one of her children. This one is mine."

His finger delicately stroked the purple stone, and damn if my heart didn't thump against my rib cage. "There were three of us, and I was the only one who took an interest in cooking, so go figure."

"It would be a good way to honor them," I murmured as I shut my eyes, lulled by the waves and sun. "You should do it more."

"What do you mean?" he asked, and though my eyes were closed, I could feel his gaze on me.

"Cook, take classes, learn from your head chef, whatever your heart desires," I said and squinted my lids open. The blush on the top of his cheeks had deepened, like I had pleased him with my words. “And then let me sample your food. I think I just thought of the way you could pay me back for filching my bike.”

I heard his deep chuckle. “That’s what this is really about—feeding you.”

I grinned. “If it works, then my job here is done.”

# 11

# WEST

We fell silent, simply enjoying the warmth of the sun, the soft rocking of the boat as the waves rolled in to shore. It felt comfortable being here with him, which was fucked up because essentially I only knew him from his grooming business and countless phone conversations.

Except I was basically trapped on a boat with him in the middle of Lake Erie, and I didn't even know how to swim. Not that he was a serial killer, for Christ's sake. Just that I had placed myself in this vulnerable situation with somebody I barely knew, and I could be more miserable right now than I actually was. In fact, I was enjoying the in-person Tristan as much as I'd enjoyed the phone Tristan, maybe even more.

The danger was that I not only enjoyed the sound of his voice, but I was attracted to him as well. So I needed to keep myself in check. I had crossed the line before with someone I felt too familiar with, and I didn't want to get sucked into the same kind of situation.

Though Tristan was much more open and compassionate than Michael ever was, and it seemed he was just trying to stay afloat after losing someone as well. There was a certain safety in that. Not only that we got each other, but that we each had our own walls up that forced us to keep a physical distance, if not also emotional.

The sun had lulled me into a false sense of sleep, but at some point, I heard Tristan stand up and fish around for something. I squinted in his direction and saw he was holding two bottles of water. He passed one of them to me before cracking his open and taking a long swig.

"Thanks." After twisting the cap, I sat up a little straighter in order to take a sip.

Tristan motioned to the back of the boat. "I'm going to jump in."

My gaze darted to the water, considering its depth and vastness, and my chest squeezed tight. "What, *here*?"

"Yeah, sure," Tristan said with a chuckle. "The lake is refreshing after baking in the sun."

I watched him warily as he walked to the boat's platform and dove over the side. I sprang up and hurried to the edge as if he'd disappear on me and leave me stranded.

He surfaced after another second, and I breathed a sigh of relief. For some strange reason, I had this immediate fear of being abandoned, which I knew was irrational. The same fear that cropped up often ever since the fire. It was unfounded but would probably always stay with me. Only recently had it occurred to me it was one of the reasons I had lived with Michael for so long. I suspected he knew that too, and I wished he hadn't preyed on it —whether unknowingly or not. I wished he'd encouraged me to spread my wings more.

But I was an adult; I couldn't really blame him for anything. Again, I reminded myself that I had made the first move in that relationship, and I didn't plan on making that mistake again. Not unless there were already set parameters—which was why hooking up worked best for me right now.

"You okay?" Tristan shouted from the water. Rivulets ran

down his face, and with his hair slicked back away from his forehead, he looked even more handsome. I'd always been drawn to older men, maybe because they always seemed more straightforward and stable, but we saw what trouble that got me in.

"Yeah, fine," I replied, but I could tell he didn't really believe me.

"Want to come in?" he asked, motioning with his arms and splashing the surface of the water.

I shifted my knee on the vinyl to a more comfortable position, as if testing the sturdiness of the boat. "I'll drown."

Had he forgotten I told him I couldn't swim?

He shrugged. "Use a life jacket."

As if it were that simple.

"I used to teach swimming at the Y, and I bet you'd learn really easily if you ever want me to show you."

I immediately began shaking my head.

He held up his hands. "Sorry. Too much, too soon?"

I nodded as my chest lightened. I liked that he was so honest and chill about stuff. There wasn't much guessing between us. If he felt something, he said it. I didn't have many friends like him. I didn't have many friends, period. So I mostly didn't want to blow this.

"I'll be right here if you want to try to jump in with the life vest," he said as he began treading water from one end of the boat to the other. "No pressure."

I sat back and watched him swim and float while he told me about kneeboarding and tubing on the lake and how exhilarating it was to be flung around the surface of the water. "You definitely have to wear a life vest for that."

When he dove under and swam a little closer to shore, I got brave. I walked to the long bench, pushed it open, and tugged one of the orange life vests out.

I slid it over my head and fastened the buckle with shaky fingers. I felt ridiculous in the puffy bright thing, but there was no one else around to judge me. The sun was beating down, the vest was sticking to my clammy chest, and suddenly the idea of being surrounded by cool water sounded refreshing.

I made my way to the stern of the boat where Tristan had returned to bobbing in the water. When he saw me, his smile was so bright and genuine, it was nearly blinding.

He didn't make me feel ashamed that I couldn't swim. He made me feel brave. Supposed he had all along.

I sat down on the edge of the platform and let my feet dangle in the water. It felt cool and soothing to my heated skin. "You sure I won't drown?"

His eyes sobered as his gaze locked on mine. "I won't let you."

My chest tightened and my breath hitched. Damn, I liked that.

"After you go under, the buoyancy of the life vest will propel you to the surface," he said. "I'll stay at arm's length to make sure."

"Is the cold water going to suck the life out of me?" I asked, staring down at the dark blue lake.

"At first it might steal your breath," he replied, splashing a little as he floated. "But now it feels awesome."

I stared down into his kind eyes as I tiptoed to the edge of the boat.

Moment of truth. Did I trust him enough to keep me afloat?

Loaded question.

# 12

# WEST

I SUPPOSED I TRUSTED TRISTAN ENOUGH TO COME ON HIS BOAT AND anchor in the middle of Lake Erie. He'd been the man who gave me an out from Michael that one night that seemed so long ago now, and he lent me his bike—well, sort of. He's been tolerating my calls. He's sort of become a friend, and a lifeline, even though I told myself I didn't need one.

He lost somebody too.

With that thought firmly in place, I teetered off the edge, took a deep breath, and jumped into the water. I was only under for a split second before the life vest boosted me back up. It was fucking cold and felt like my lungs had turned into ice cubes.

I gasped and scrambled, my arms flailing in momentary panic until I felt strong hands—one on my arm, the other on my shoulder—anchoring me.

I bobbed up above the surface and sputtered water as my breathing evened out.

"You good?" Tristan said behind me. "I knew the jacket would be fine but didn't want you to feel like you were drowning."

I nodded, unable to speak right then, sort of embarrassed that I freaked, though I knew Tristan wouldn't make light of it.

Another few seconds more and Tristan's hands released me, and though I logically knew at this point I wouldn't drown because of the life vest keeping me afloat, I had the urge to tug his arms back around for an extra layer of support.

He swam around in a semicircle so that he was facing me. He smiled, braced my shoulder momentarily to steady me, and then we were bobbing together.

From directly on top of the water, Lake Erie looked so vast—like it had the potential to swallow you up. Before I freaked again, I swung around to look at the shoreline instead and saw all the people on the beach as well as on rafts, along with a couple of lifeguards.

"Holy shit, this is amazing," I finally said, realizing that I was actually swimming in one of the five Great Lakes. Well, not exactly swimming—but maybe someday.

"Isn't it?" Tristan replied. "I think we take for granted that we live on this surprisingly large body of water."

We treaded water for a while, talking about random stuff like work and cooking, my roommates, and Tristan's employees, whom he considered family.

After we got back on the boat, he pulled anchor, and we headed toward the breakwall and then to his slip on the dock. It felt like we were returning from a great adventure instead of a simple boat ride on Lake Erie.

We'd only been out on the water for a few hours, but the sun had a way of draining all your energy. Almost like I needed a nap.

I assisted Tristan by tossing the rope toward the metal cleats on the dock like he instructed me and then securing it the best I could. Tristan had jumped out on the other side and helped tow the boat closer so he could wind the rope around way better than I ever could. "I'll show you how to tie a knot sometime if you want."

Some unnamed emotion slid weirdly inside my chest. First

the offer to teach me to swim, then to tie a knot. Guess we really were becoming friends.

Once I helped him snap the large black cover over the boat, I headed to my bike and loosened the chain on the post. We walked together along the dock toward the parking lot.

"Feel like getting a burger and beer at the tiki bar right there?"

I glanced to where he pointed, and there was music, and people eating at outdoor picnic tables, as well as a bar in the center of the grass. "Sounds perfect. I'm starved."

We found an empty picnic table where I leaned my bike; after we sat down, a server greeted us immediately, and we ordered burgers and beers. The atmosphere was casual, the company just right, and fuck, it felt like one of the best days I've had in a very long time, if ever.

"Thank you," Tristan said in such a sincere voice, it made me pause with the beer halfway to my mouth.

"For what?"

He shrugged, but a timid smile lined his lips. And maybe it was the sun and the beer, but it looked damn good on him. It made me want to lean forward and take his mouth in gratitude. I had no idea what had come over me right then.

"For spending the day with me," he said and shyly looked away. "It's been a while since I've been out here. You helped me christen the boat."

"Not a problem. It was fun," I replied, meeting his eyes, which had softened at the corners.

After we finished our food and drinks, we headed toward the parking lot, and the idea of getting on my bike and riding home made my body sag in not only weariness but melancholy. I wasn't exactly ready for the day to end, but I knew it was time.

We paused near his truck, the same automobile I'd sat in weeks ago after I'd made a life-changing decision. "I could always..." He motioned to my bike and the back of his car, but I was already shaking my head. "Only because it's been a long day and you're tired, I swear."

I gripped the handlebars, considering swinging my leg over the seat and riding off without a second thought. I was sure to feel more energized with the wind at my back.

"You don't even have to show me where you live," he said in a pacifying voice. "If that's what you're nervous about."

Damn, how did he know? I wavered, deliberating, my knuckles turning white.

What was the harm? By this point, I knew Tristan. He wouldn't break my trust, would he? And if he did, I'd lose his number in a hot minute, right after I gave him a piece of my mind.

"Okay," I conceded, wheeling the bike toward his hatchback.

He helped lift the ten-speed in the back, and then I sank onto the passenger side and he was driving me home. "Where to?"

My pulse sped up. "I don't...*please*—I don't want Michael to know."

"Of course not," he replied. "I wouldn't. You have my word."

I studied his eyes a long moment before I said, "Head toward the Ohio City area."

He nodded, turned right out of the parking lot, and kept driving. Once we got to the intersection of 25th and Bridge Avenue, I motioned toward the corner of the street.

"You can just drop me off here," I said in a rush as my gut throbbed because I had let someone get this close to my truth.

"Sounds good," he said, not batting an eyelash, probably figuring I wouldn't dare take him directly to my apartment. But now he knew the general neighborhood.

My stomach squeezed tight. I could trust him to leave my business alone. He'd proven that thus far.

After he popped the hatchback, he helped me haul the bike out of the vehicle.

"Thanks," I said, looking away as my cheeks fired up. With the way I was acting, I could easily understand why he might've once thought Michael was hurting me. Hopefully by now he realized that the man was intense and the only way to get my life back was to make it a clean break.

"Not a problem." Tristan only looked briefly in my direction before he waved and slid back inside his truck. Probably assuming I'd need him to leave first, he stepped on the gas and inched into traffic. He didn't even glance in the rearview mirror to see which direction I'd be heading, and damn, I respected him for that.

When he got about two streetlights away, I climbed on the bike and turned west toward my apartment, marveling at the awesome day I had.

## 13

## TRISTAN

I PLACED THE STANDARD POODLE IN THE HOLDING PEN AND RUBBED him behind the ears. All week long my thoughts had drifted to West, playing our day on the boat over in my head. It was difficult to pinpoint how I felt being around him in person. On the phone it was comfortable, two disembodied voices, getting to know one another without the pressure of outside influences. In person, it was fun. Exciting. Way more personal.

But everything seemed to change after that Sunday. Nothing momentous occurred while we sunbathed side by side on the boat and then floated comfortably in the water. And yet somehow the ground between us had shifted in an essential way. I had enjoyed my time with West, and unless I was reading too much into it, the feeling seemed to be mutual.

I wouldn't lie and say I wasn't feeling a buzz of attraction in my stomach the entire time as well, because it was definitely there. West was adorable, charming even. To experience this kind of excitement about somebody felt thrilling but also surreal and a bit sad, like I was betraying Chris. My heart pounded against my rib cage. *I'm sorry.*

But I needed to ask myself if West's appeal was a result of the fact that I hadn't been around a guy I was attracted to—a guy who absolutely intrigued me—for that many hours in *years*.

Regardless, it was fruitless to give it any more credence since this was such an unusual circumstance. West was attempting to find his own footing for the first time in his adult life. He had lost his entire family in a tragic way, and even though Michael had been kind enough to take him in, it had turned into something unhealthy. And given how careful he was about keeping the details of his new life close to his vest, it made me wonder if there wasn't something I was missing in all this.

As I led the chocolate lab to the shampoo sink, I pondered it further. If Michael found out where West worked or lived, what would be the worst of it? Was West afraid he'd be influenced into returning to his life with Michael? Was Michael that convincing? He definitely had an overbearing personality, and from the little West gave away, he influenced a lot of the decisions West had made. Those red flags were enough to convince me to keep my distance and instead offer West the solace of a friendship he seemed to crave.

The week flew by with an influx of appointments most likely due to folks heading on vacation and wanting their dog groomed.

"Another person looking for boarding," Elijah said after he got off the phone with a customer.

We'd been asked about lodging for pets several times this summer, and Elijah had begun offering weekend rates on the side. He would take one or two dogs home with him at a time for an overnight stay for a preset fee. His roommate, Nick, was cool with it, especially since he mostly stayed at Brin's place. But apparently the idea had put a bug up Stewart's ass, which of course had led to more disagreements between him and Elijah.

But I was happy that Elijah was finally taking the initiative on something. He had also mentioned reenrolling in classes at the community college, having dropped out in his early twenties.

A couple of generic texts from West before or after his shifts were the only contact we had since the boat ride. And maybe it had given both our brains a bit of a reprieve. I certainly didn't want him to read into anything. It was more important he felt comfortable confiding in me and considering me a new friend. It would be wrong to think of him as anything else. And honestly, I wouldn't want anything more either. Even though it was almost three years since Chris passed away, my life was just beginning to feel less numb without him.

Friday evening after closing time my cell buzzed with a text from West. **What are you up to?**

**Just about to close up shop and head home. You?**

**My roommate and I are heading to a club tonight.**

My stomach squeezed tight as I imagined West dancing with sexy men and having a good time. My club days were long gone.

**Clubbing, huh? That's perfect for you.**

I waited on his response as the last customer picked up her dog and I finished sanitizing the shampoo basin.

**Why is it perfect?**

I tied up the garbage bag and locked the door behind me, then fired off my response.

**Because you're young and you should go out and have fun.**

I took the trash to the Dumpster and mentally planned the rest of my night. Walk Mack around the block and then make myself something to eat, which would more than likely consist of a frozen dinner.

**How about you?** West asked as I walked to the car.

**What do you mean?** I replied as I slid into the seat.

**Don't you go out anymore?**

I smiled. **Not to clubs. Haven't been in years.**

**Isn't it time for you to start living?** I could just see the smirk on his face.

**Ha, touché,** I replied and then shifted the gear into Drive to head home. I thought about whether or not I was living or existing. But that was what a devastating loss did to you. My employees really helped pick up the slack at work while Chris went through chemo and radiation, and afterward, I'd show up at work just to go through the motions because I was completely lost otherwise.

As I pulled into my lot, my phone pinged again. **Why don't you meet us there?**

**I don't think so,** I replied quickly.

**C'mon. Maybe it'll be fun...and we can both find a hookup.**

My gut churned. Was that the reason he was going to a club? I didn't know why it bothered me—he might've been hooking up left and right all along. Just because he called or texted me every few days didn't mean he didn't have somebody in his bed all the other times.

**Suppose I always hoped it would happen organically with somebody. But maybe not anymore.** I liked keeping it honest between us. It was better that way.

**Not unless you consider Grindr and clubs organic, old man.**

I laughed. **Oh, I'll get you back for that.**

**You'd have to see me to get me back. So you'll come?**

**Maybe,** I replied, getting out of the car and walking inside the building.

**I hear a yes in there somewhere.**

I wasn't sure why he was being so insistent.

**Maybe. You trying to teach this old dog some new tricks?**

I had just put the key in the lock when he replied.

**I'm not the only one that needs to find myself again.**

I sucked in a deep breath. Fuck. I bent down to greet Mack, whom I'd kept home today. When I left him this morning, he seemed content gnawing the bone on his pillow near the glass sliding doors.

**We'll be at Kiss in Tremont at ten,** he replied.

**Ten?** I typed. **I'll be in bed.**

**My point exactly,** was his response, along with a funny-face emoji.

**We'll see. If I don't show, let me know how it was.**

After I walked Mack along the back of the property to do his business, I made myself some mac and cheese from a box because that was my existence. It made me remember that I wanted to ask West whether he cooked for himself or his roommates or brought home stuff from the restaurant.

Why in the hell was I always thinking of him?

And that was the other thing—did I really want to go to a club only to stand there alone while he hooked up with somebody?

*Well, why not? He considers me a friend, nothing more. I should be able to do that for him. Just be there, hang out, and go home.*

Around a quarter to ten, I almost changed into my pajama pants but instead found myself tugging on different clothes. A pair of tighter jeans that Chris loved on me. My heart thudded in my chest.

"What do you think, Chris? Do you approve of me going to a club?" I asked the empty room.

*About time you got off your ass*, he'd whispered the morning I went to the boat dock.

*You've got a lot of years left*, he'd told me a week before he passed away. *Promise you'll find someone to love again. Don't be alone.*

I forced the thought from my brain before I was tempted to slide inside my sheets and curl up in a ball, too grief-stricken to go anywhere. I was already a jumble of nerves.

Instead, I fished through my closet for a tighter-fitting T-shirt. I put gel in my hair but left the scruff on my chin. Elijah and Brooke had told me it was hot. *Christ.*

Maybe a hookup would do me good as well. Except that wasn't exactly me. I'd probably only fallen for Chris because we were friends first. I tended to need the emotional connection first.

Ah, fuck it. What the hell did I have to lose? I hadn't been touched in so long, I wasn't even sure my cock worked properly.

*Liar*, Chris huffed out. *It worked just fine the other night when you were imagining skinny-dipping with a certain twenty-something.*

## 14

# WEST

Marco and I stood at the bar, taking it all in. The sweaty bodies, the thumping music, and gorgeous men everywhere. So why was I so preoccupied with looking toward the entrance?

I had already danced with one guy who had his hands all over me, and I let him have his way because it felt good. But damn if I didn't need something more. Sometimes I even craved it. Close contact with somebody. Strong arms, warm breath. Sometimes I longed for it more than anything else.

I'd had my share of hookups, men with their hands and mouths on me, but that was only temporary, and after both of us were satiated, the night was over.

Michael wasn't a cuddler, and I was too embarrassed to admit that I was looking for some nurturing—something I'd been missing ever since my family had perished in that fire. But I was a grown-ass man, and I had gotten away from Michael and that whole situation because I wanted to spread my wings. So it was silly to want something so basic. But I absolutely did sometimes; it was like a hollow ache deep in my bones. Except that wasn't something you put in a Grindr profile.

I noticed him the moment he walked through the door.

Tristan looked around, his jeans and shirt fitting him perfectly, his hair styled to a tee. He'd come here with his game-face on, and it made me grin. As he walked through the space, I noticed plenty of eyes on him, and something else stirred inside me. I was attracted to him. But I wanted his companionship more. No way could it be anything else anyway. Not while we were both so lost. Clinging to each other for anything other than friendship might lead down a road neither of us was prepared for. The timing was terrible, but that was life.

"Look at that fine piece of ass. Not quite a bear or daddy, maybe more like an otter," Marco remarked as Tristan neared. He loved zeroing in on the type of guy he wanted to hook up with for the night. I kept from rolling my eyes.

I raised my hand in a wave. "That's my friend Tristan."

"Hot damn," Marco muttered as I introduced him to Tristan, who gave him a quick once-over, and my stomach clenched; I wondered if he was interested as well. Fuck, that would be awkward. But then Tristan turned his full gaze on me, and a sexy smile quirked his lips.

"What are you drinking?" he asked as he motioned toward the bar.

"Whatever's on draft," I replied, and Marco nodded.

Tristan ordered drinks for the three of us, and just as he turned to hand them away, Marco was approached by a tall man who had been giving him the eye earlier.

As Marco went off to dance, Tristan smiled and sipped his drink.

"You don't look so out of place as you made it sound, old man."

"Guess it's like riding a bike." He winked. "Comes back to you."

I arched an eyebrow. "Cruising, or being out in this setting?"

"I was never much for cruising," he said. "How about you? Any prospects?"

Just as he said the words, the man I danced with earlier walked up and asked if I wanted to join him again. When I looked at Tristan, he winked, giving me the green light that I wasn't being rude. Except I was torn as the guy led me toward the thumping music—he might be a possibility for later tonight, but I also wanted to stay and talk to my friend.

Once we got to the dance floor, I could feel Tristan's gaze on me the entire time, and for some reason that made me want to shake my ass more seductively.

What the hell was I doing? The man got all my wires crossed.

After a few minutes, I looked over my shoulder and noticed a gorgeous man chatting Tristan up. I swallowed roughly. *Good for him.* He coaxed a reluctant Tristan toward the center of the floor. Tristan's cheeks became flushed as soon as he began moving his hips to the beat, and I was mesmerized. He wasn't bad at all. The man grabbed onto his waist, and I was having trouble keeping my eyes on my own dance partner.

After the man's hands started roaming and Tristan let him grope his chest freely, my cock stirred to life. But when the guy suddenly grabbed his face and kissed him, that was apparently Tristan's hard limit. He allowed it at first but then pushed back and swiped at his lips with his forearm. He shook his head, and the guy seemed to mouth *my bad*.

My dance partner and I headed back to the bar while Tristan stayed out there through a couple more songs. The guy he was with still gripped his hip, but he had stepped back and kept his distance.

"You want to get out of here?" my dance partner whispered in my ear. The smell of his cologne was a little strong, but he was definitely attractive and we might just have some good chemistry together.

"I'll let you know in a few," I replied, my gaze searching the dance floor again for Tristan. "Let me hang with my friends for a bit longer."

As he made a beeline for the restroom, I looked around the large warehouse-style space, immediately spotting Marco making out hot and heavy with someone in the corner. Out of the corner of my eye I noticed Tristan walking toward me, sweat dripping off his forehead.

"Told you you'd have fun," I teased.

He smiled while softly panting through his nose as he ordered a second drink and settled beside me. "Guess you were right."

"Maybe you'll invite somebody home," I replied even though the idea of it made my pulse kick up a notch.

"Not really my thing. Not that there's anything wrong with that." His gaze tracked around the dance floor. "Where did your guy run off to?"

"Dunno," I replied, sweeping the bathroom area for him. "He asked to get out of here. But I'm not sure."

"Why not?" His eyebrows knitted together. "Not your type?"

"It's not that," I replied, not sure why I was sharing. Except it just seemed to come naturally with Tristan. "I've had my share of hookups, but I guess I'm...just hoping for something different."

"What do you mean?" Tristan asked as heat crawled across my neck.

I shook my head, suddenly wishing I hadn't opened my mouth. "Never mind."

I could feel him studying me as I watched a table of rowdy guys in the corner of the room.

"Some kind of kink?" he asked low into my ear, and I shivered from the intimate feel of his warm breath. "Nothing wrong with that."

"Oh yeah?" I asked, and when I met his gaze, the tops of his cheeks were rosy. "Nah, nothing like that." Squaring my shoulders, I took a reinforcing breath. "Just want...someone to sleep with me."

"What?" he asked, leaning toward me again like he didn't hear me correctly. I could smell his cologne. A light floral scent mixed with sweat. It was much more appealing to my senses that my dance partner's, but I shoved that out of my brain.

I've admitted plenty to Tristan by now, so what was one more thing? "I sort of miss...cuddling with someone."

He drew back to look me squarely in the eye. "You're not looking for sex?"

"Not exactly." I chewed on the inside of my cheek. "If it happens, cool. But I just want someone to hold me."

"Christ," he said, taking a huge breath, looking completely flustered, if the blush crawling across his cheeks was any indication. "Okay, listen, if you just need to cuddle and you're not too grossed out by an old man, I'll hold you no strings attached. You don't need some dude to stick his dick in you."

My mouth dropped open, and then I swallowed several times in a row, trying to wrap my brain around his offer. But Tristan didn't look embarrassed, only concerned.

"What if I want to stick my dick in *them*?" I asked with an arched eyebrow.

"Holy shit," he said and gripped the counter. "You are full of surprises."

"Yeah...guys generally get that wrong. Not all twinks want to bottom."

Unfortunately, it was a desire I conceded when I just wanted to get my rocks off. But those opportunities were too few and far between for me lately.

Tristan crossed his arms. "And not all bears want to top. Not that I'm a bear, just telling you I understand the point."

I chuckled. "Marco pegged you as more of an otter."

His gaze flitted toward the dance floor as if scouting around for Marco. "Christ, these boxes we put ourselves in. Can't we just be attracted to people's hearts?"

Damn, it was the perfect Tristan response.

I clinked my glass against his and our eyes snagged and held, as if we'd each learned something new about the other. I needed to get my dick to stop pushing up against my zipper, because holy fuck, did Tristan have layers to him that I unexpectedly longed to peel back.

"It's totally natural to miss somebody after they're gone," he remarked. "So the cuddling actually makes sense."

I shook my head rapidly. "Michael wasn't a cuddler. I just..."

His eyes were wide and searching. "I think I get it. No need to explain more."

Suddenly the guy I'd been dancing with earlier turned up with two friends. We all talked for a bit, and then the man encircled my waist and whispered in my ear, "Let's get out of here."

My gaze met Tristan's, and I noticed how his throat worked to swallow. But then he winked at me again and smiled, as if telling me to go for it.

We said our goodbyes, and as we began walking toward the exit, Tristan grasped my arm. "Do me a favor and let me know you're safe tomorrow? Or whenever?"

"Yeah, sure," I said as my shoulders tensed up. But I couldn't compare his concern to how Michael always checked up on me. This was different. This was Tristan not only being a gentleman, but also a friend.

# 15

## TRISTAN

After West left, I felt sort of deflated, even though I could've actually gone home with someone as well if I wanted. Or in the bathroom as was offered to me by my earlier dance partner. *You want to fuck me? Then let me suck you off.*

Maybe in my heyday, when Chris and I were only friends and went clubbing together, but now it just felt too impersonal.

I thought of West's words. *Not all twinks want to bottom.*

Holy Christ, now I'd have that on repeat in my head. And that was bad news. I had opened my mouth and probably said the very thing to make him freak, which was so stupid of me. He decided to leave with somebody else anyway. I downed my drink and headed for the exit, looking forward to crawling into my own sheets, alone.

What the hell had I been thinking coming here? Except it did feel good to dance and be wanted by someone, even if it was just for a quickie.

When I got outside, I was stunned to see West standing against the wall near the exit. I looked around but didn't see the guy he had left with.

"What are you doing?" I asked, glancing up and down the street again.

"I…dunno," he said and had trouble meeting my eyes.

"What happened to your hookup?" I placed my hand on his shoulder, wondering if something bad had transpired. "Did he—"

"Can I still take you up on that offer?" he asked unexpectedly, and my heart thumped hard against my chest. "I just… I changed my mind, is all."

"About leaving with him?" I asked.

"Yeah… I mean… I guess what you suggested sounded nicer."

Damn, my pulse was beating unsteadily against my throat.

"Yeah?" I asked, leaning against the wall alongside him. "How come?"

"You said no strings attached?" he asked in a shy voice, and he sounded so earnest that I had trouble not reaching out to him right then and there. Instead, I kept my distance so as to not make him feel crowded.

"Of course," I replied in a thick voice, still having trouble believing we were actually having this conversation. "You want to be held, then I'll hold you for as long as you like."

What the fuck was I doing? But he looked so young and vulnerable right then that I figured I'd made the right decision. We could be adults about this. Wanting affection was not a sin, after all.

"Better not stand here and deliberate," I said, suddenly feeling all kinds of antsy. "Let's walk to the car, and if you change your mind, I'll drive you home instead."

He followed behind me, and when I stopped long enough for him to catch up, I attempted to decipher whether he regretted his decision. But given the rosy coloring in his cheeks, he was simply uncomfortable, and I certainly didn't want him to feel that way.

After we slid inside my truck and I began driving to my condo, I started wondering if I needed this as much as he did. He stared out the window the entire time it took to get to the freeway. My heart thumped as I speculated whether he was gearing up to change his mind and preferred to be driven to his neighborhood instead.

So I turned the radio up and pretended to hum a random song to give him some time to think. When I passed the exit that would've been the route to take him home and he hadn't said a word, I let out the breath I'd been holding.

As my shoulders relaxed, I glanced over at him. He was still tense, his hands in fists on his lap.

"Hey, you freaking on me?" I asked in a light voice. "I can turn the car right around; it's no big thing."

"It's just… I don't want to be indebted to anyone," he replied, finally making eye contact with me. "I want to be free to choose who I spend time with."

"Absolutely," I agreed, wondering where this conversation was headed. "You wouldn't owe me anything, West. I promise."

He glanced at me and held my gaze for a moment.

"I get that maybe you feel safer with me because we've sort of become friends, but you still don't owe me anything," I explained, driving the point home, but he still looked wound tight. "And I definitely won't break your trust by telling Michael."

He gasped like I'd read his mind, and had I known that'd been in the back of his brain this whole time, I would've voiced it sooner. "No matter what happens. Even if you decide you're done talking and hanging with me, and Michael happens to show up again to ask about you, I wouldn't."

His fists unwound, and he placed his palms on his thighs. "Why?"

"Because you're allowed to break up with somebody and live your own life."

He nodded as he fished his lip through his teeth.

"Can I ask you a question?" I said as I exited on Lake Avenue, headed west toward my condo.

"Okay..." he replied unsteadily.

"Why does it freak you out so much that Michael might find you? Is there something that as a friend...I should know?"

"He's just...a very persistent man, and I felt under his thumb," he confided. "I'm starting to like my life, however shitty it may seem to somebody outside looking in. I'm making minimum wage, living in a crappy apartment with two roommates, and I've got no wheels except for this bike I hocked from..." He peered at me from under his long black lashes. "Well, from some cool guy I now consider a friend."

I smiled at that. Damn, he was adorable.

"It's everything Michael snubs his nose at...but it's all finally mine, you know?"

"I actually get it," I replied. "That's exactly how I felt when I ultimately aged out of that group home and was on my own. It was scary, sure, but liberating too."

A small smile lined his lips like we had one more thing in common. "I just don't want Michael showing up like some knight in shining armor trying to rescue the pitiful princess stuck in the tower."

"Understood," I replied, pulling inside the parking lot to my condo.

"Not that there's anything wrong with being a princess," he mumbled, and I laughed. "I'd just rather be the kind that doesn't need the prince on a rescue mission."

"Okay, princess, that makes sense to me," I replied as I shifted the car into Park. "And don't worry, I have zero prince qualities." He grinned at me in an endearing way that made my heart beat funny. "We cool now?"

"Yeah," he replied, reaching for his door handle.

"It's late. Let's not think any harder about this," I said as I met him on the sidewalk. "Let's just go to bed."

He inhaled a sharp breath as my pulse throbbed in my neck.

After we rode the elevator and stepped inside the apartment, we each took turns petting Mack, who eagerly greeted us with a wagging tail.

Feeling tired yet also lit up at the same time, I headed into the bedroom to change into a pair of pajamas. I left on my T-shirt and fished another pair from my drawer. I met West in the living room, where he was standing near the sliding glass doors, staring out at the dark lake. I handed him the bottoms, knowing they might be large on him. "You can wear these if you want."

He slid them from my fingers and went into the bathroom to change. When he emerged, he was carrying his jeans folded over his arm and had also left his shirt on.

We both seemed to sober suddenly, and the air around us grew thick with tension, even though we'd been in this scenario before. Although last time he'd slept on my sofa, and he was certainly free to do so again. If he changed his mind, I didn't want him to feel bad.

"I'm exhausted," I said. "Going to bed. Again, no pressure if you'd rather stay on the couch."

I climbed into my bed and could feel his eyes on me in the doorway. I lifted Mack to the end where he normally slept and shut my eyes, giving him an out. The darkness helped my shoulders relax and my breathing to even out.

About a minute later, I sensed West draw back the covers on the opposite side as he slid into the sheets.

As soon as I felt his body heat beside me on the mattress, a shiver raced through me. I craved this so goddamn much, I realized, maybe even as deeply as him. Hot tears sprang to my eyes, but I swallowed rapidly and forced them away. Still, I couldn't help trembling all over.

I heard West gasp, and when I opened my eyes, he was staring at me. I blinked several times to become adjusted to the darkness; the faint light from the lamp in the living room helped.

"It, uh, hadn't occurred to me that you also... I didn't mean to..." His hand swept around the bedroom. "Have you never..."

Fuck, this was not something I wanted to talk about right now. No, I hadn't had anyone in my bed since Chris passed away.

"Don't. It's okay. I wouldn't have asked you if I didn't mean it." Our eyes met in the dark room. "Come'mere."

He cautiously slid toward me, and as I drew him into my arms, all I could think was that he smelled good—like rosemary and lemons. His head landed on my neck, and as I enveloped all his warm skin, I heard him sigh. And fuck, did that make my heart pound loudly inside my chest.

"This okay?" he mumbled against my throat. West's warm arms wound around my neck, and it was my turn to sigh. Damn, it felt so good. Too good.

When he shifted to align our bodies, I could feel his cock lengthening against my hip, and goddamn, from the outline, it seemed huge. *Fucking hell.*

He swore under his breath and tried to angle away, but I held on tighter. "S'okay. Just a physical reaction."

As West settled against me in bed, my shaft instantly grew to a semi. I ignored the sensation, my fingers stroking through his hair as I attempted to soothe him—and me as well. Soothe the boy who lost everything and the man who was desperate for a new start. He moaned into my shoulder as my fingernails lightly scratched his scalp.

"So good," he murmured, and in another minute he was fast asleep in my arms.

With the heat of our bodies wrapped so perfectly together, it didn't take me long to drift off as well. One of the last things I remembered was West's soft hair brushing against my chin, and feeling a contentment I hadn't experienced in a long time.

My fingers drifted to the pulse point on his neck and rested there, just to be sure his heart was beating, that this was in fact real. I ignored the memory of feeling for Chris's pulse every day and night as he lay dying in the hospice. Sure, it was an image that haunted me, but that wasn't what this was. This was about a living and breathing guy who had been through an ordeal and needed comfort—comfort I was all too willing to give.

*I could get used to this.* I sighed before I quickly swept it away.

This was one night and one night only.

Sometime near dawn, I dreamed of swimming in the lake with Chris, who then morphed into West, his wet bangs sticking to his forehead, his eyelashes beading with water, and a sweet smile on his face.

I woke up in a sweat, gasping at how real the dream seemed. As I shifted against my pillow, I realized that my arms were as empty as my bed. Disappointment and longing surged through me at the loss.

But it wasn't like I'd actually believed in the fantasy of waking up with West and sharing a pot of coffee while viewing the lake from the balcony...

Just as I suspected, the pajama pants I lent West were neatly folded near Mack on the end of the bed, and West was gone.

## 16

# WEST

I PARKED MYSELF NEAR ANOTHER BUSBOY AT THE SERVER STATION, listening to the staff complain about the glut of customers waiting to be seated. A group of animated men sat at table number fourteen, closest to one of the large front windows, and I clenched my fist, waiting for them to leave so I could speedily bus the table for the next group of diners. When I had gone to fill their drink glasses for the millionth time, one of the men, who had briefly made eye contact with me, looked me up and down like I was nothing more than a piece of gum stuck to the bottom of his shoe, and it made my stomach turn—people who felt entitled, and in this case, men who were taking up space even though they'd long been done eating.

It was the exact sort of thing I'd watched Michael do out in public with any number of people in the service industry—valets, bussers, dry cleaners, and tailors of his immaculate suits. Even at my last job that Michael hooked me up with under the guise of helping me out—and maybe even keeping an eye on me or trying to have a hand in crafting my future—I'd notice things. How he'd treat assistants or security at the front desk. Even me, now that I thought about it. Even though he was fucking me, I was still only an office clerk, and he was the king of the castle—or finance department, as it were.

As I bussed a different table vacated by men and women dressed business casual, I thought about how I was never allowed to mention my intimacy with Michael to any coworkers—it would be unprofessional, he'd told me. Instead, he'd inform people I was a friend of the family, which wasn't too far off, I supposed. But because employees thought I was aligned with him, they'd continued to speak in hushed tones when I was near or would abruptly pause the conversation as if I'd out them for talking shit.

It placed me in an awkward position, for example when he'd call me into his office to do something, like sort through his mail; it made it seem as if I was receiving special treatment, which made it even worse. Other times he'd tell me to lock the door or stay late to organize the files or any number of things, and at first, I'd admit it was exciting. Like sneaking around with the boss.

He'd ask me to pull his cock out of his pants and blow him, which I now realized was some sort of fantasy for him, but the whole experience would leave me feeling on edge. Coworkers would side-eye me as if they knew the real story, and it made me increasingly uncomfortable. I didn't make any friends for fear of spilling the beans, and now finally being out from under his shadow, I could see how wrong it all was. How much he'd manipulated the situation to his benefit.

That was why I couldn't let him know where I was, so when Tristan had asked me that very question, it was difficult to explain. Except he got it, of course he did—he knew Michael as a customer. Michael had reduced him to merely a person who serviced him as well—or rather his dogs. The very idea of Michael snubbing his nose at someone as cool and wonderful as Tristan made my stomach pitch.

At home, Michael and I would get into arguments about his arrogance. I'd tell him he was being self-righteous, and he'd tell me I needed to be more discerning with my tastes. He'd almost convinced me that we could have an awesome life filled with material things. That he'd show me how to make good money, and that we'd travel the world together. But with each passing day, I'd felt more and more like his boy toy. A kept man, without a backbone. I took a good hard look in the mirror and asked myself if this was what my mom and grandma would want for me. I heard my mom's voice in my head.

*Jonas West Hollis, what do you want from this life? Having money helps, but it's not what fulfills a person. We don't have much, but you kids make me happy.*

My grandmother would add something of her own.

*Go after what you want. Work hard, but always be kind.*

And when I looked at Michael, all I saw was the opposite of everything they stood for. And that was when I knew I'd had enough.

As table fourteen finally paid the check and stood to leave, I saw the same man pass the other busboy his valet ticket, and I barely kept from rolling my eyes—as if he couldn't wait five minutes for his own damn car. As soon as the group made it to the lobby, I descended on the table, noticed the measly tip they left for the hardworking server, and began clearing the dishes.

Near closing time, the manager pulled me aside, and at first I thought I'd made some sort of misstep. "West, we're going to be down a server next month. Would you like to begin training for that position? I can put you on the same schedule as Marco."

Marco would tell me I'd make good tips and eventually I could afford some decent wheels.

"Can I think about it?" I asked, glancing toward the kitchen door. I was bummed about possibly losing time with the chefs.

About once a week, the sous chef requested I help in the kitchen, either at the salad station or with washing dishes. It didn't matter as long as I was part of the experience. I had even gotten comfortable enough to speak to one line cook, named Tony, about culinary school.

"There are a couple different schools of thought," he explained as the other cooks got into a heated debate about it. A few of them had attended one local school or another, but some had not, and they argued that it took several years under an experienced chef, not a high-priced degree, to earn your chops.

"You keep impressing me with your work ethic, and I'll teach you some things," Tony had said and glanced at the one prep cook who was always tardy. "You already got a jump start on a couple of other lazybones around here."

I nodded and kept my head down, more than appreciative for the offer.

---

I WAS SO CONFLICTED ABOUT THE MANAGER'S PROPOSAL THAT I texted Tristan as soon as I got home and was lying in bed.

**If I take a server position, I'd make tips, but then I might lose my time in the kitchen, and Tony said he could teach me some things.**

His response was what I'd expect from Tristan. Calm and thoughtful.

**Ask yourself what you want more, and stick with it.**

He worked it through with me, which was exactly what I needed.

**But shouldn't I be thinking about money right now? I don't even own a car, just a shitty bike.**

I imagined him smirking at the inside joke. *Our* inside joke. Whoa, how had that happened?

**You might actually enjoy working as a server. Sometimes you don't know until you try. Maybe talk to the manager about doing both?**

Damn, I loved working things through with him.

**True. Maybe I should tell him how much I like being in the kitchen.**

**There you go.**

It was refreshing that he didn't try to throw money at me or solve my problems. He was acting like a friend and just listened to me. And that was what made me want to seek him out even more.

Despite the attraction.

For the hundredth time, I couldn't help deliberating about my sleepover with Tristan. I'd instantly melted into his warm arms as he wound them around me, as well as into his cool sheets, which were better than my cheaper, scratchier ones. But I couldn't think that way. That would've been Michael's logic, and those things didn't matter.

So what did matter, exactly? That was what I was working through, and I had all the time in the world. I had no parameters, and Tristan was a guy I had developed a cool friendship with, nothing more. If you didn't count the boner I'd popped.

*S'okay. Just a physical reaction.*

He'd gotten one too, and my body had turned into electric heat as I thought about rubbing our groins together. Had it been a hookup, there would have been no question that getting off was the end goal. Not cuddling afterward—that wasn't a given, not like it was with Tristan—and I was so desperate for it that I'd tossed jerking off straight out of my mind.

Tristan instantly felt different than Michael, which was a plus. Michael never felt quite right to me; not that Tristan did—he was just a warm body. Wasn't he? But that vulnerability I'd seen in his eyes when I slid into the sheets... Fuck, that had done something to me.

Had I been the first guy since his partner died? Damn, that would be huge for a man like Tristan, but I couldn't allow my brain to go there—it was too overwhelming to even consider. Besides, he'd seen me vulnerable as well.

He'd known how much I wanted it, needed it, and had welcomed me with open arms. It was the exact reason I needed to leave his apartment before he stirred and it felt too awkward between us.

My eyes focused back on my cell.

**Besides,** Tristan had added. **I might benefit from your new cooking skills.**

**You asking me to feed you?**

**Better than leftover pizza and frozen dinners.**

**True. Someone needs to make you eat more nutritiously. I mean, I'm poor, but I still aim for fresh fruits and vegetables.**

**I try! And fail miserably.**

**I can help you.**

**Thanks.**

**What do I get in return?**

I didn't know why I said it. We were heading dangerously into flirting territory, and I was afraid he would take it that way.

**Whatever you want.**

Fuck, I couldn't breathe. I grew an instant boner that I pushed down with the heel of my hand. I couldn't—shouldn't—think of Tristan that way. But before I could respond, he connected the dots and took us in a different direction. Always respecting my boundaries.

**How about another day on the boat, and I teach you to swim?**

**Thinking on it.**

**You can feed me after. If you want. That can be our trade-off.**

I didn't respond for five whole minutes, my heart beating out of my chest just considering it. I wanted to—fuck, I wanted to. But that might be crossing the line. Probably sensing my hesitation, he responded to me instead.

**Don't think about it too hard. It doesn't have to be a real offer. I just made it since I'll be at the boat on Sunday again.**

**I'm not saying no.**

**Good. Gotta get to bed. Have a good rest of your week.**

And just like that he gave me another out. He let me breathe, and that was what I liked about him. There was no pressure. And it reminded me of the kind of friendship I used to have with this kid in school before everything went to shit.

Damn, I hadn't thought about Danny in a long while—not since he tried to contact me a couple of years ago and Michael discouraged it, saying it would only bring back the nightmares I had my first year after the fire.

Danny and I used to spend time at each other's houses, shooting the breeze and jacking off together in his room. He felt comfortable and safe. And fuck if that wasn't exactly what I was feeling with Tristan right now.

And suddenly I wanted Tristan so badly in that moment that everything ached—my heart, my stomach, my groin. The pain of frustrated longing was sharp, digging into my chest and practically carving out a hole.

Feeling feverish, I tore off the covers. My hand slipped inside my boxers, my fist found my cock, and I began stroking painstakingly slowly, root to tip, thinking about how Danny and I never touched, just watched each other.

Then Danny morphed into Tristan. I imagined telling him to pull his cock out and pressing up against his warm and slick body, tasting the tang of his tongue in my mouth. Ordering him to bend over so I could see his hole and play with it. In my fantasy, he was game and eager to please me. *Not all bears want to top. Not that I'm a bear, just telling you I understand the point.*

My fist pumped faster and harder as I thought about the noises that might come out of his mouth. Calm, unruffled, and reserved Tristan panting and begging me for more.

Holy fuck. I shot hard onto my stomach, my hand sticky with my come.

Damn, I was in so much trouble.

## 17

# TRISTAN

Friday night I met the guys at Bent, our neighborhood bar, because I felt like I wanted to get out of my apartment and stop ruminating over West. And yet, I almost invited him. Almost. But I didn't want to be disappointed if he didn't show. Or if he did show and went home with somebody else. I couldn't beg him to cuddle with me again, even though I wanted to, badly.

Instead I met Brin and Nick, Elijah and Stewart, as well as Elijah's friend Kam out at the bar. I think I surprised them all by showing up for the first time in months. But it felt good to just cut loose and laugh.

Except when I spotted Michael cruising the bar, I knew I'd made the right choice by not inviting West. Michael was on the other side of the room, talking to some tall guy, who looked just as pretentious as him in nice pants and a button-down shirt, minus the jacket and tie, as if they'd both just left a late night at work. That guy seemed more his type, so the idea of him being with West really threw me for a loop.

But when you actually understood how it happened, how they'd known each other for years, and how West had made the first move, it made sense. Plus, given Michael's sanctimonious attitude about life in general, it seemed, maybe he felt more secure being in a position of power over West. Probably why West felt nearly defenseless by the time he left him. At least that was what I'd put together in my head about that mess of a situation.

Elijah nudged me. "Look who's here."

"Damn," Brin said. "That's a first, so he must be desperate."

"Or lonely," I muttered, and even though I wasn't indicating myself, Nick frowned at me. I shrugged because it was close enough to the truth, so I just rolled with it.

"Think he's hoping to spot his ex here?" Elijah asked.

"Maybe," I replied, and though I'd told the guys that West and I had spoken several times on the phone—that we had become friends of sorts—that was where I stopped short because they would hound me about it and I definitely wanted to give West his privacy.

But that wasn't the whole truth. The whole truth was that I sort of wanted to keep West for myself. I looked forward to our texts and conversations, and especially to the opportunity to see him again and spend time with him. It was hard not to think about how he felt in my arms or how his steady pulse point felt against my fingertips.

A while later, I was standing with Kam near the bar, talking to him about needing a new bike, when I saw the guy Michael had been talking to go off to dance and Michael making a beeline for me. Fuck.

"What's up?" I asked as he approached. Given the relaxed tie at his neck, I was positive he was still wearing his suit from a day of work, and though there were certainly men who liked the crisp, buttoned-up look, he also stood out because of it.

Michael attempted to appear nonchalant, but from the gleam of sweat on his upper lip, I could tell he was on edge—either from spotting me or being in a gay bar, I wasn't sure which.

He looked around at who might overhear our conversation, before leaning forward. "Have you—"

"No," I remarked right away to get it over with. "And even if I had, what business would it be of yours?"

His eyes narrowed at me. "Like I said before, just want to make sure he's okay."

I shook my head. "That all it is?"

He stared at me for a long moment before his shoulders dropped, and he chewed on the inside of his lip, looking the most vulnerable I'd seen him.

"You miss him," I stated as plainly as possible. "It's okay to feel that. I miss somebody too."

My finger automatically twisted my wedding ring around, and his gaze followed the motion. It made me wonder if he was one of those men who wore a ring or if he opted not to. I studied his hand even though it'd been years since his divorce.

"Just feels strange without him after all this time," he replied, stuffing his hands in his pockets. "Same with the new place I'm taking Coco and Chloe."

It'd been so long, it was almost hard to associate those two pugs with him. "They doing okay?"

"As ornery as ever. Just like..." He sighed. "Trying to figure a way to find him. He left some things at my place."

I straightened from the stool I was leaning against, upset with myself that I'd let my guard down with this man. West had told me he was... What was the word he used? Resourceful? Or was it persistent?

"Why would you do that? If he wants his stuff, he'll ask for it, don't you think?" And suddenly it became even clearer to me why West was so freaked about Michael knowing anything. This was a big enough city to lose yourself in, thankfully.

Had he put his ex-wife through this same bullshit?

"Want the chance to see him too. If I could just talk some sense into him, he might want to—"

"Might want to what?" I asked, attempting to control my outrage.

"He had a good life with me," he said, straightening to full height. "I know how to take care of him."

I shook my head. "Maybe he just wanted the opportunity to take care of himself."

Right then I felt my phone buzz in my pocket, and I had a strong suspicion it was West, but I didn't dare pull it out in front of Michael.

"How do you know that? Have you talked to him?" he asked, his face turning into a scowl. He looked me up and down as if assessing me, much like he'd done other times.

"I told you I haven't." I rolled my eyes, which made him tighten his jaw further. "Christ, let it go already."

I kept my lips in a neat straight line even though I could've said so much more.

"Maybe find yourself someone new to save," I bit out, though I knew it was absolutely the wrong thing to say. He bristled at my statement. "There are plenty of prospects here for you."

Not that I'd wish that on anybody.

"*You'd* never be one of them," he said, and I chuckled, like his words humored me. Which only made him angrier.

"Yeah, whatever." I motioned with my hand. "Go fuck yourself."

When he stormed off, Kam gaped at me. "What a character."

"Tell me about it," I muttered as I watched him head toward the other end of the bar. Fuck, that whole conversation had put me on edge. Made me want to protect West even though he'd want no part of it.

My gaze swept the club and landed on Brin and Nick, who were passionately making out in the center of the bar, and damn if that didn't make my heart stir. Stewart had dragged Elijah off the dance floor, and they were arguing about something in the corner, which only made me tense up again.

"And then there's Stewart," Kam remarked, motioning to them. "He could probably be that Michael guy's brother."

I winced. "He's not putting his hands on him, is he?"

Kam shook his head. "I don't think so, but damn, Elijah deserves better."

My eyes again swept toward Brin and Nick. "Think we need an intervention?"

"Maybe. Thing is, he's got to come to his own conclusion. We all have to," he said with some pain in his voice, and I knew he was referring to his own breakup that Elijah had told me about earlier in the year.

I sighed. "Hope it's soon."

After the guys returned to get something to drink, I fished my cell out of my pocket, figuring it was safe.

**You asleep?** West had texted.

I smiled as I typed. **I'll have you know I'm at a club.**

**What? And you didn't invite me?**

**I'm with a bunch of friends. Would you have wanted me to?**

**Maybe.**

**I'll have to remember that for next time.**

I deliberated about sharing my conversation with Michael, but I was one for honesty.

**Probably a good idea you didn't because Michael was here.**

There was silence for a long beat, so I filled in more details.

**I spoke briefly to him. And no, I didn't mention that you and I are friends.**

Finally, he responded. **Thank you.**

**And I understand a bit more now why you don't want him to know.**

**You do?** he asked.

**He's pretty...intense.** And plenty of other things I didn't want to type.

**Can we talk?** Even though we were texting, I could tell my seeing Michael made him anxious.

**I'll call you in five when I'm walking out.**

I said goodbye to my friends, pulling Elijah aside before heading for the door.

"I know Brin has already talked to you, and I'm sure you're not going to want to listen to me," I whispered in his ear. "But maybe you guys need a break. Time away to think about some things."

Surprisingly, he nodded, and his shoulders dropped in defeat. I patted him on the back. "You can talk to me anytime. I'm just a phone call away."

As I strode toward the exit, I spotted Michael in a darker corner with a short and lean guy. Michael had him pressed against the wall, his lips on his neck. Guess it didn't take him long. Or maybe it was all for show. Maybe he was hoping I'd see him and somehow let West know. But damn, I did not want to play any kind of games; that was not me.

When I called West on the way to my car, he answered on the first ring.

"Think he was looking for me?" he asked in a nervous voice. "Because he never stepped foot in gay bars—at least not with me. Too repressed for that."

"Not sure," I answered honestly. "But he certainly wanted to know if I'd been in contact with you again."

And after I recounted the bulk of my conversation with Michael and we said our good-nights, I felt deflated. Like seeing Michael had put a huge damper on my friendship with West. As if a black cloud was hanging over what we had built. West would probably be more cautious as a result and not as willing to see me in person. That was why continuing to harbor fantasies and an unhealthy attraction to him was risky territory.

Maybe he was only in my life so we could help each other through some hard times. I should be grateful if that were the case. Thankful that he got me back to doing some of the things I'd enjoyed before Chris got sick and passed away. If that were all that ever came of this, then I'd find it in me to be happy. Maybe even join a dating site, see who was out there. Possibly go on some boat trips with some other guys. Even though the idea of it didn't sit right with me in this moment, that could definitely change in the future. You just never knew.

*Right, Chris? I can do this.*

His answer came in the form of the wind whistling through the trees as I pulled up to my condo and headed inside alone. *You're stronger than you think.*

# 18

# WEST

As I wheeled my bike along the dock to the slip, I froze. Tristan was standing on the walkway, helping a couple of women off the boat. I had a sneaking suspicion I knew exactly who his company was, and now I felt like I was intruding.

Fuck, I knew I shouldn't have come. All my self-doubt this morning should've sent a warning flag. Ever since Tristan told me he'd run into Michael, I knew I was taking unnecessary risks seeking him out. But I couldn't seem to stay away.

I'd convinced myself that Tristan running into him at a club the other night had been pure coincidence. They did live on the same side of town after all, and there weren't *that* many gay bars in the city. Michael had told him he'd been looking for me, which didn't surprise me, and even though Michael never stepped foot in such an establishment when he was with me, he might've assumed I'd be there by chance.

Besides, Michael was used to having things right at his fingertips, and my leaving him had been another giant blow to his ego. I'd seen how agitated he'd been when his wife walked out, and at the time I'd felt sorry for him. Now I questioned exactly what went down those weeks after. I remembered their bitter arguments over the phone because apparently, he'd been a stubborn bastard during divorce proceedings.

Unfortunately, Serena could give two shits about me, even though she'd agreed to have a sixteen-year-old who'd lost his entire family live in her home. I felt some sort of strange solidarity with her now. Would things be different if she'd given a damn? She could never replace my mother or grandmother, but it would've been nice to have her support.

Before Tristan and the two women could spot me, I spun my bike around and headed in the opposite direction, but I was too late.

"You made it," Tristan exclaimed.

When I turned toward him, an adorable, almost boyish grin lifted Tristan's lips as relief flitted through his eyes, which made my heart thump wildly.

The women looked between the two of us, their eyebrows raised, as if they couldn't register the connection. I couldn't blame them; I never would've imagined my friendship with Tristan either.

"Um, West, this is Judy and Sheri, Chris's mom and sister," he said as he shifted awkwardly between us. "It's a beautiful day today, so I took them for a spin around the breakwall."

Chris's family, holy shit, my suspicions were right. Meeting them felt strange, almost wrong. Except Tristan and I were only acquaintances.

Chris's mom smiled. "Poor Tristan. Chris and I never wanted to go on the open water, but Tristan has always been a good sport about it."

"No worries," he said with a wink. "I'm just glad you came."

"Did you know my brother?" Chris's sister asked as she studied me a little too closely. She looked down at my bike, and something seemed to register for her as well.

I shook my head. "I, uh, only through Tristan's stories about their life together."

Her eyes softened as she looked between us, and Tristan shifted uncomfortably under her scrutiny.

"I'm going to walk them to the parking lot," Tristan said abruptly, as if to get them moving. "Feel free to wait for me on the boat."

He strode down the dock, and they followed, saying their goodbyes as they passed, but my feet felt cemented to the wooden plank as I watched Chris's mom link arms with Tristan. *They're my family too.*

Up to this point our real lives hadn't intersected.

Except that wasn't exactly true because Tristan met my roommate Marco the other night at the club. But Marco was such a new and cursory addition to my life; we had no history or shared past. Not like Tristan had with Chris's family.

But Tristan did have contact with Michael, a few too many times in fact.

Suddenly everything felt way too intimate, but before I could reason my way through it, Tristan was already walking back to the boat. "I know what you're thinking."

"I don't think you do," I replied, my hands clenching the handlebars. "They... That's Chris's family."

"I told you we were close," he replied, and when I opened my mouth to offer some sort of lame protest to why coming here was a bad idea, he added, "I'm allowed to have friends. So are you. They don't begrudge me that."

"Do they know how we—"

"I said I knew you from the grooming business, which is not a lie."

My shoulders unwound. He was right; I was being ridiculous. Why did it matter? Tristan and I were only friends. Sure, we'd shared a bed the other night, but that had been pure need and didn't ever have to happen again.

*So why do I want it to?*

"Sorry," I mumbled. "It just felt important. Them being here. Me showing up."

"They *are* important to me. They always will be," he replied, exhaling. "But so are my friends."

Our eyes met and held as his meaning exploded in my brain. He was saying that I was becoming important to him. That he cared. And the words washed over me like a salve, but they also made me want to climb on the bike and get the hell away from all the feelings pressing in on me. I realized I wanted to matter to Tristan. Because he was beginning to matter to me too. Big-time.

He broke eye contact and began walking toward the slip. I silently followed, and after I chained my bike up to the post and stepped inside the boat, I instantly felt my body relax, even though all my nerve endings were still buzzing.

"Glad you came," Tristan said, opening the cooler and pulling out two waters.

"Me too," I replied as he handed me a cold bottle.

"Want to head out?" he asked after unscrewing the cap and taking a swig. "We don't have to think about anything else; we can just ride."

I nodded, feeling calm and contented. He had that effect on me. He took the pressure off, even though I'd already begun stressing hours ago.

Just like last time, I helped him untie the ropes from the dock, and we quietly motored past the breakwall. I sat down on the cushioned seat across from him and held on to the side of the boat as he sped up. Tristan rode out on the open water parallel with the interstate to the east side of town before he decided to double back. It felt invigorating as the wind whipped through my hair and the sun beat down on my shoulders.

Once we got back to the west side, he glanced over at me. His cheeks were rosy from the wind, his hair in disarray, but he looked happy, and that made my stomach flip-flop—the idea that I had been part of a nice day on the water with him.

"Want to anchor and float for a while, or do you need to head home? Either way is fine."

The idea of drifting and relaxing was one of the things I was looking forward to on this outing with Tristan, and I'd been hoping he'd ask. "I'd love to."

"Cool," Tristan replied with a smile as he motored toward Edgewater Beach just like last time. After he set anchor, we took turns slathering suntan lotion on ourselves, and when his fingers stroked over my back, I held back a shiver. I liked when he touched me. It was human contact, after all.

After we relaxed against the seats across from each other, we talked about random things. I told him about helping Tony in the kitchen, and he told me about the employees he considered family. The idea of having people around that I considered good friends or relatives tugged at something deep in my gut. Maybe someday I'd have that too.

I fingered my necklace, and he zeroed in on the motion. "Tell me about them?"

"Who?" I asked.

"Your siblings," he replied, and I sucked in a breath.

So I did, and I found it didn't hurt quite so much telling him how my younger twin sisters, Ella and Elaina, were tied at the hip and rarely apart. How they were goofballs and loved to jump on my back and ask for horsey rides.

His eyes softened as he listened. "Where do you think they are now? Do you believe in an afterlife?"

"Do you?" I asked as my heart slammed against my chest.

He twisted his wedding band around his finger like he always did. "Dunno. I like to think so. That Chris is healthy and somewhere safe. I talk to him sometimes and imagine he answers me. It sort of helps...keep me grounded and sane."

"Yeah...yeah, me too," I admitted. "I think the hard part for me is that I didn't have a warning, no time at all to say goodbye. They were just *gone*."

Our eyes met and held. "Yeah, I hear you. But saying goodbye was fucking brutal, and watching him wither away..." He squeezed his eyes shut and shook his head.

I had never considered that part of it. If that was the case, then in some ways maybe I was more fortunate. But fuck that, no one is lucky with death.

"Guess there's no easy way," I remarked. "It all sucks."

"Big-time," he replied, nodding. And then his eyebrow arched as if he'd thought of something else. "How about your father?"

"Never knew him. He passed when I was little," I replied. "His last name was Hollis, and my mother's maiden name was...er, West."

"Your real name is Jonas," he said matter-of-factly, and my jaw dropped open. "That first day that Michael came looking for you, I called you West, and he was bowled over."

I grimaced. "Bet he was. It just felt...*right* to use it."

"It suits you," he replied. "It's another way to honor her. Your grandmother too."

My chest felt lighter. Damn, he got me.

"*Your* parents?" I inquired.

It was a question I'd wanted to ask back when Tristan first told me he'd been in the foster care system. What kind of parents would leave a defenseless kid in the system without working to get him back? I gritted my teeth, unsure if I wanted the answer.

"Thankfully I was too young to remember, only pieces and parts, like my mom's hair was this wheat-blonde color," he replied, pushing back his wavy bangs from his forehead. I pondered if he resembled her, even though his hair was darker with a hint of auburn.

We were quite the pair, I thought, as the boat continued to rock from the light wind rolling off the lake. Being in the middle of the expansive lake made me feel so small, almost inconsequential. But talking to Tristan made me feel as essential as the very air we breathed.

When Tristan got hot enough to dive into the lake, I watched him for a while from my perch as the boat gently lulled me. He didn't mention teaching me to swim, and part of me wondered if he'd changed his mind. But more than likely, he was only giving me space. The fact that I could read him that well overwhelmed me a bit. But it also made me feel safe and protected—he'd had that effect on me from the moment I got in his car that night.

"Just let me know when you're ready to take off," he said from the water.

I peered over the side at him. "Whatever happened to those swim lessons?"

His eyebrows rose in surprise. "Anytime you want. Just say the word."

Feeling brave, I stood up. "How about now?"

He smiled. "Perfect."

"Should I wear a vest?" I asked, lifting the seat cushion I'd just vacated.

"You can at first, if it'll make you feel comfortable."

The idea of going without felt scary and enticing all at once.

But for now, I'd opt for safety first. "Promise you won't let me drown?"

"If I did, I'd miss out on whatever meal you promised as payback," he replied with a smirk. "And believe me, I'm all for that."

A nervous laugh jumped from my throat, even though the idea of cooking for him—for anybody, really—thrilled me. I pulled the sticky orange life vest over my neck and fastened it, figuring I'd bob around at first and get used to the water.

After I jumped in, I stuck close to Tristan, still nervous that I'd somehow float away from him and feel abandoned in this giant body of water.

"You ready to try without the life vest?" he asked in a tentative voice.

My pulse pitched, but I still nodded. I knew he wouldn't leave me stranded or let anything happen to me.

"We'll just practice floating."

Tugging me closer to the edge of the boat, he helped unsnap the vest. As he fished it over my shoulders, his gaze met mine. "It's okay. I got you."

He placed the vest on the platform, where my fingers were digging into the edge for dear life.

Tristan moved behind me, his hands winding around my waist, and I immediately felt goose bumps line my skin. Just like I did when I was lying in bed with him. His lips found my ear, and it made all the hair along my nape stand on end. "Breathe, West. It's going to be okay."

I nodded as I inhaled through my nose and panted harshly through my mouth.

He placed his fingers precariously around my nape as he directed me. "I want you to lie back in the water. We're just going to float. Once you get the hang of that, the rest is easy."

I lifted my legs and attempted to do as he instructed as one of his hands gently cupped my skull and the other, the small of my back. After several failed attempts, I was finally able to drift on the surface of the water with his assistance. "Holy shit, it's working."

He chuckled. "It is. Tread the water with your arms."

I followed his instructions and felt like I was accomplishing something.

"Once I release you, you'll probably feel like you're sinking, but that's when you've got to think about staying suspended above water. You ready?"

I took a deep breath and nodded. He slowly withdrew one hand and then the second from beneath me and backed an inch away from me.

I felt the strange sensation of my stomach swooping as I

gently treaded water with my arms to keep me afloat. "I'm doing it."

He nodded. "You definitely are."

As soon as I said the words, I began sinking, and panic set in almost immediately. But Tristan didn't even allow my head to get below the waterline before he grabbed me around the waist and pulled me tightly against him.

"I got you," he murmured against the side of my neck.

I relaxed instantly inside his arms, and we remained silent as I caught my breath and my heartbeat settled down. But Tristan's crotch was right up against the crease of my ass, and I could feel him steadily filling. His breathing became erratic as I grew a semi along with him, right smack in the middle of Lake Erie.

Neither of us uttered a word, and I could almost hear Tristan whispering, *S'okay. It's a physical reaction.* Still, I didn't want him to let me go, and as I placed my hands over his and pulled him firmly around me, a soft gasp released from his throat.

My cock hardened instantly. I leaned back against his shoulder, and I could feel his soft breath on my neck. I had the urge to angle my head, to look in his eyes, to brush my lips against his. Were they as soft as they looked? Would his irises reflect the same desire as mine? But I was terrified of being wrong, of going too far, of bursting this bubble of perfection we were floating in right now.

I couldn't remember the last time I felt like this, like a pure kind of happiness buried deep inside my soul was bubbling up inside me, forcing its way out. I felt free and alive, wanting to stay right here in this moment with Tristan.

"I think we're probably done with the lesson," he murmured as his heartbeat thumped wildly against my back.

Without looking at him, I nodded. He swam backward, taking me with him, and as soon as his shoulders touched the platform, his arm released me, jolting me back to reality.

He flipped us around so I was the one to grab hold of the boat first. “You ready?” he asked in a soft voice.

“Ready,” I replied as he let go, and I pulled myself onto the platform. As we dried off with the towels he’d retrieved from the cabin, we both looked elsewhere, even though I was curious to see if he was still sporting an erection.

Once he pulled anchor and began motoring back to the slips, I finally breathed more freely. Holy shit.

After I helped him dock and we were back on dry land, I unlocked my bike from the post. “Thank you,” I said, finally meeting his gaze.

His eyes crinkled with a smile as if we’d shared something cool, great, *intimate*. “Not a problem.”

As we began walking toward the parking lot, I pushed the words past my lips before I chickened out. “Feel like eating?”

He breathed out as if in relief. “What do you have in mind?”

“Drive me to the grocery store, and I’ll surprise you.”

# 19

# TRISTAN

After we loaded the bike in the back of my truck, we drove to the nearest grocery store off Clifton Avenue in comfortable silence, the sun having taken a beating on us. It was hard to put my finger on what exactly happened between us today.

He not only shared more of his history with me, he'd also trusted me enough to be in Lake Erie without a life jacket. And when I'd felt myself grow hard against him, I wanted to pull away and act as if nothing happened. But then I heard his breath catch and noticed his flushed cheeks, as if he were as turned on as me. Of course, it could've been some sort of primal physical reaction, but damn if I didn't want to stay there with him for even longer, holding him right up against me. Everyone needed human contact from time to time, and it had been so long since I felt that way with somebody, like I was glowing and vibrating from the inside.

If he'd been too uncomfortable or turned off, I would've expected him to pull away from me. Unless he'd felt too vulnerable in the water without a life jacket. Fuck. Had I placed him in a position he didn't want to be in with me? But by the way he'd briefly glanced my way, first at my eyes and then at my mouth, I'd gotten the impression he craved the closeness as much as I did. Hadn't he slept in my bed for just that reason?

Except if either of us had decided to make a move, it might've ruined everything. And I enjoyed his company way too much to scare him off. No chance I wanted him to feel like it was a repeat of what he'd had with Michael.

When West first arrived on the dock, he was freaked by seeing Chris's family, and they were a bit rattled as well—especially since Sheri immediately noticed my bike. She was always good with details. As I walked them to the parking lot, I explained that I was letting him borrow it for the summer, and didn't share anything beyond that.

But I could see it plainly in their eyes, and it nearly gutted me —they questioned whether I was moving on, leaving Chris behind, and nothing could be further from the truth. I could never say goodbye to him—he lived inside my heart. If ever there came a time somebody new stirred that fragile place, soothed its damaged surface, I'd have to make room. It was unlikely such a thing would happen anytime soon, if ever. Some people only ever found one great love in their lives.

In the store, I noticed how West warily searched around the aisles, and it finally occurred to me that he was in close proximity to the neighborhood he used to live in with Michael. Shit.

"Did you and Michael ever grocery-shop here?" I asked him near the seafood counter.

"No," he replied, his gaze shifting over my shoulder. "But ever since you told me about running into him at the bar, I've been wondering when and where he might show up."

"Say he did—just for kicks," I asked, lowering my voice. "What would you do?"

His eyes grew wide. "Leave as fast as I could."

"Without saying anything? Did you ever consider he might need to hear it again, that it might help?" I asked as West reached for a package of fresh seafood and placed it in the basket. "Would it help if you called him and put your foot down? Told him again that you're done?"

"Guess I'm just not ready for that. He's too tied to everything that's painful about my past, and I know I'm avoiding it, but I don't want to go there, not yet. Not ever, if I can help it." He shook his head while his fingers skimmed over a row of bottles in the wine aisle. I bit my tongue instead of pointing out that the more you try to avoid something, the more you'll be forced to face it. I thought getting rid of most of Chris's possessions would lessen the blow, but it did no such thing. I was forced to work directly through my grief; there were never any shortcuts.

"Not sure he'd really hear me anyway," West remarked. "He can be pretty determined—and persuasive."

I picked up a bottle of red and studied it. "Unless he hooks up with somebody else?"

"That actually might help." I winced, and he caught my reaction before I could turn away. "What?"

"I, uh, saw him with a guy, in the corner of the bar, before I left the other night," I replied in a tentative voice, not sure how he'd feel about that. "So maybe he's been getting out more?"

"Could be," he said, and I heard relief in his voice. "Unless it was just for show. He's all about impressions."

"Yeah, I'm starting to realize that," I muttered as I placed a bottle of red and another white in the cart. It felt so domestic shopping with him. I missed that feeling with Chris, when we'd go together and divide the list. But I needed to be careful and not read too much into it.

We stood in the checkout line with a basket that contained salmon, asparagus, lemons, and wine.

I knew if I offered to pay, he wouldn't accept it. So instead I placed a twenty-dollar bill down on the conveyor belt and proposed to split the grocery bill.

"I want to pay you back...for the bike...and the lessons," he replied with pleading eyes. "*Please.*"

My stomach balled tight at his sincere expression. When I finally nodded, he released a breathy pant.

---

After we got home, I took Mack for a walk while West used my shower to rinse off from our dip in the lake. Once back inside, I found him in the kitchen already prepping the meal, digging through my cupboards for spices. His wet hair was dark and curling near his ears, and I wanted to reach out and touch it.

I watched for a while as he methodically salted the salmon and asparagus. Then I used the bathroom to take my own shower.

We ate the fantastic dinner out on my balcony with a view of the lake and skyline. "This is perfect, thank you."

West blushed. "It actually feels good to cook for somebody, so thank *you*. Though your spices are lacking, mister. We need to correct that, stat."

I laughed even as a shiver raced through me at the implication that he planned to cook for me again.

"Don't I know it," I muttered. "What does the kitchen in your apartment look like?"

He made a face. "I live with two other dudes."

"*Spotless*, then?" I replied, and he chuckled, the grin lighting up his whole face. I wished I could see him smile more often. Or at least hear it in his voice, since I was more used to his tone than his face. But damn if it didn't feel nice having somebody here in my place, enjoying a meal with me.

When I reached for the wine bottle and tried to top off his glass, he raised his hand to ward me off. "I shouldn't. I have to ride home."

We had chained his bike to the rack outside the condo for the night.

I couldn't help feeling disappointment heavy in my chest, but

I tried to temper it with some humor. "No cuddling session tonight?"

He arched an eyebrow in my direction. "Are you making fun of me?"

"Absolutely not," I replied as our gazes snagged and held. "That night…helped me too."

He swallowed roughly. "Helped you how?"

"Dunno…" I responded, breaking eye contact, and looking down at my plate. "Helped me sleep better, I suppose. Like I was connected to someone."

He pushed back from the table an inch. "It didn't bother you that I was…in his bed?"

My eyebrows climbed to my hairline. West thought he was invading the sacred space I'd shared with Chris? Could that be why he left at dawn—because it was too hard to face me in the morning?

"Actually," I replied, wiping my mouth with the napkin and tossing it down on my empty plate, "I bought an entirely new bedroom set the year after he passed. I couldn't…"

My throat clogged with emotion as my elbows sank to my knees.

"No need to explain," he replied in a distressed voice. "Damn, I get it."

My eyes met his, and I could see that he really did get it. But maybe he also questioned how I could do such a thing. His entire family perished in a fire—what mementoes did he get to hold on to?

I stood up and began clearing dishes, hoping a change of subject or scenery would be better. He helped me load the dishwasher, and then we sat down on the couch, where I topped off my wineglass from the bottle, leaving his nearly empty. He didn't object, so maybe he'd decided it was time to get on the road. Still, I didn't want to play any guessing games with him.

"Does it make you feel better knowing it's not the same bed?"

I asked, trying to address the elephant in the room again. My thumb moved to the wedding band on my finger, but I stopped myself from twisting it. I pondered if the ring also threw him off. It hadn't even occurred to me to take it off. Until now.

*Fuck. This is hard, Chris.*

"Yes and no," West replied in a soft voice. His gaze drifted to the photograph of Chris and me on the side table. It was of us on our ten-year anniversary at Pier W restaurant. He had requested a table with a view of the water for *me*.

It made me realize how many leftover reminders of my life with Chris I had kept around. If West had been able to save anything, would he have done the same? My gaze zoomed to his neck, where I could just make out the silver chain peeking above his collar.

"What's the no part?" I asked gently.

"Huh?" His eyes searched mine.

"You said yes and no," I reminded him. "What's the no part?"

He sighed. "I don't want to like it—the cuddling. With you."

"Why not?" I asked, my hand sliding to his knee in a gesture of support. I could feel him trembling. Ah, hell.

"I don't... I can't..." He motioned back and forth between us. "Not when I'm just finding my way on my own."

"I understand," I replied, squeezing his knee and then removing my fingers. "So maybe we can be adults about this."

"What do you mean?" His fingers caught my hand and moved it back in place on his knee. My heart stuttered.

"If one of us needs something, we ask for it with no strings," I replied, entwining our fingers. "I won't pretend to know what this is between us. Maybe we're supposed to be in each other's lives for a reason—like to help us through tough times."

When my thumb slid along his palm, he shivered. Damn. "All I know is I like it—being with you. Holding you."

"I like it too," he murmured, his fingers grazing over mine. I tried to control my runaway breaths. Just a simple touch from him made my heart race.

"I'm not sure I believe any of that kismet shit, though," he said with a smirk. "Even still, you'd do that? With...no strings?"

I shrugged as my fingers brushed over my wedding band, and his eyes followed the motion. "As you can tell, I'm not that much further along than you. *Except...*"

"Except what?" he asked, anxiety lacing through his eyes.

"You'd have plenty of people to meet your needs if you just continued to..." I waved my hand, unable to find the right words. "Put yourself out there."

"So would you," he countered, his eyebrow arching.

"I'm not..." I shook my head. And before I could get the words *interested* or *ready* out of my mouth, he disputed me again.

"Neither am I," he replied as his fingers grazed over my palm, sending shockwaves racing through my spine and all along the fine hairs on my legs. "For now, just want to be with you. That okay?"

My heart clogged my throat. It'd been so long since somebody said those words to me, even if he did mean no strings attached. "Yeah...I want that too."

Now that we'd established some ground rules, I noticed how West allowed his gaze to linger over me longer, in sweeping glances. How much he might've cautioned himself from looking his fill before. His gaze traveled all around my face, from my eyes to my lips and down to my neck and chest. Longing filled his eyes, but something else as well. Maybe admiration, as if he liked the way I looked, and damn if that wasn't intoxicating, having his full attention on me now.

I looked my fill as well, appreciating his sculpted cheekbones and gorgeously long eyelashes, his full lips and the soft waves of his hair. I wanted to reach out and touch him, skim my thumb across his jaw, but I kept myself in check for now.

"So...where does that leave us?" I murmured in a tentative voice.

He bit his lip as his gaze locked on mine, and damn if he wasn't the most adorable thing I'd seen on the planet. Fuck, he did things to me, and I needed to cut it out before I was left alone and disappointed. But the way he held my fingers and teasingly scraped his nails along my wrist, I was practically panting from the contact.

"With more wine and a bed to cuddle in?" he asked, and I barked out a laugh.

I picked up the bottle and finally topped off his glass. Before he took a long gulp, he said, "Cheers."

## 20

# WEST

AS I SETTLED AGAINST TRISTAN BENEATH THE COVERS, WITH MACK at our feet, I had that same feeling of comfort and peace as that other night, yet different. As he wound his arms around me, his larger body surrounding me, I was also thrumming with excitement and a fuckton of desire. This time we ditched the idea of pajamas but kept our underwear on, and feeling his bare skin next to mine was so much better. Warm and smooth with patches of fuzz along his chest and upper thighs that tickled my back and legs. I wished I could stay enveloped in his strong arms for days.

He sighed against my ear, and I couldn't resist squirming and shifting against him, my head landing against his neck so I could smell him. Warm and spicy from that soap I used in his shower. My cock instantly stirred against his thigh, and this time I didn't get embarrassed or try to pull away. His fingers stroked through my hair, and I could feel him rousing as well.

I adjusted my leg over his, avoiding grinding up against him even though I desperately wanted to. Tristan was so calm and reasonable; what would he look like coming apart at the seams?

*If one of us needs something, we ask for it with no strings.*

"So, you know I like snuggling," I murmured into his throat, thinking about our conversation at the club that one night. "And *fucking*."

"Who doesn't?" he replied with a throaty laugh as my cock dug into his hip.

I drew back to glance at him as my eyes adjusted to the darkness. "No, I mean I love topping. Sticking my cock inside another man is the hottest fucking thing."

"Damn, that's sexy." Tristan groaned. "Thanks a lot for the visual."

"You're welcome," I replied, chuckling. But it was more than that. I enjoyed giving somebody else pleasure using my body. I felt powerful. Sensual. It helped me gain some sense of control in the vortex of my life. Not that there'd been too many opportunities, until now.

"I just wondered..." I murmured. "At the bar, you mentioned..."

"Yes," he said, without me having to spell it out. "I like to bottom, sometimes crave it. Maybe we shouldn't have this conversation while we are lying in my bed."

My fingers traced through the light smattering of hair on his chest. I was dying to know something more about him. "What do you like about it?"

His fingers skimmed below my chin. "Letting go and just feeling. I know there's power in being a bottom, but I enjoy allowing someone else to run the show. Might be why you prefer the opposite—makes sense, really."

Now it was my turn to moan as his fingernails lightly scratched against my scalp.

"What else do you like?" I whispered as all my nerve endings thrummed with electric energy. We were skating dangerously close to rutting against each other. I felt his cock lengthen against my hip, but as he shifted to entangle our bodies more closely, I knew neither of us was going anywhere.

His breaths were releasing in short pants, and when he remained silent, I thought maybe he wasn't going to answer me.

"Kissing," he finally murmured. "I like kissing."

My heart tripped inside my chest. Somehow, I just knew he'd have some romantic ideal. I almost groaned out loud, but I kept myself in check.

When I glanced up at him, the tension between us was palpable. From the moonlight glinting through the large window, I could just make out his pupils, wide and glittering with sheer longing.

"Show me," I whispered, suddenly feeling feverish, tingles rushing up and down my spine.

"Show you what?" he replied, swallowing roughly, his fingers pausing on my shoulder.

"How you like to kiss," I whispered as my heartbeat thundered in my ears. I was terrified he wouldn't be on the same page. That our lips meeting might be too intimate, too close, too much of everything, but I couldn't see past my aching desire for him.

He shivered. "West, we probably shouldn't—"

"Damn it, Tristan," I rumbled. "We just laid out the parameters after dinner. So unless you want to take something back, please fucking kiss me."

Without another word, he gripped my face in his hands, gentle yet commanding all at once. Our eyes met and held in a powerful exchange right before he crushed his mouth to mine. I moaned into the kiss because it was all-consuming in a way I hadn't ever felt before. Like some sort of visceral need was finally unleashed and he planned to devour me.

He pulled my bottom lip into his mouth and sucked on it before soothing it with his tongue. As his fingers tightened in my hair, his tongue slicked across the seam of my lips, and I whimpered as I opened for him. The tips of our tongues brushed fleetingly before he changed course, licking and nipping along my jawline to my ear and sucking the lobe into his mouth. I hummed low in my throat.

"Fuck," he whispered in a pained voice. "Goddamn it, West."

And then his mouth was on me again, his tongue pushing past my lips, stroking against mine in arousing flicks that made all the nerve endings in my body prickle. Holy shit, Tristan knew how to kiss. It was as if my request had unlocked something inside him, and I was all on board.

He flipped me onto my back and straddled me, our cocks brushing alongside each other through the thin material of our briefs. He took my mouth hostage as he licked and nipped my lips and feathered along my jaw, sucking the tender skin at my collarbone before soothing it with his tongue.

He groaned as he consumed me, stealing my breath, and I felt like I might combust at a moment's notice.

He tasted like wine and butter, and I loved feeling the weight of him on top of me.

My fingers glided down his spine to his ass, and I clutched his firm cheeks, aligned our cocks as he thrust his hips, moaning low in his throat. My balls filled to bursting point as he slid his groin against mine, and my thighs quivered beneath him.

He kissed me so hard, I thought my lips would bruise, but fuck if I wanted him to stop. I squirmed against him, begging in my own way for more.

But just as I thought he would give it to me, he changed course and slowed way down, drawing back to give us both time to breathe.

He gathered my face in his hands, and this time his lips were gentle enough to make my toes curl. His kiss was slow, his tongue brushing so tenderly, it practically melted me from the inside. His groin pressed into mine in a seductive way, making my eyes roll in the back of my head.

Suddenly the only thing in the world I cared about was the hunger that surged up inside me, arresting and torrential, like some primal rousing inside my chest, breaking the dam that had held back fear and uncertainty and grief. It was more dangerous and irrefutable than anything I'd ever felt for anyone before.

"Want you to pull me out," I groaned in a needy voice, and when our eyes met, a profound understanding passed between us.

He reached for the waistband of my briefs and tugged them down my hips.

"Fuck," he gasped. "I just knew your cock would be gorgeous."

"You're gonna make me come," I moaned, because the way his eyes drank me in so appreciatively lit a match inside me. "Wanna see you too."

He drew back and pushed his briefs down, revealing his cock, long and stiff, the head engorged and leaking from his arousal. Surrounded by that thick thatch of hair at his groin, it was mouthwatering.

"Holy shit, Tristan. I need to feel you," I pleaded.

He sank back down, and when our bare cocks aligned, I moaned, it felt so good. My legs hooked around his thighs, encouraging him to move. He thrust our cocks together, making strings of come drip from my shaft. It provided the perfect friction as my fingernails bit into the small of his back, making him groan louder.

"Take us in your hand," I begged, my breaths labored.

"I won't last," Tristan replied in a rough voice as his fist encircled us. "It's been a while."

He stroked up and down, igniting frissons of heat in my groin, causing my balls to draw up. I watched him—his wide eyes, his mouth open in bliss—suddenly glad I could give this to him. My fingers reached up to stroke along his jaw and circle his ear.

He leaned down to take my mouth again, his tongue thrusting deep, all-consuming. He kissed me through his orgasm, gasping into my mouth, and I swallowed his moans, feeling his come splash on my stomach. His hand faltered on our cocks, but I wasn't far behind, groaning and spilling over his hand, dripping down to my groin.

He collapsed on top, our lips meeting lazily for long and languid kisses.

I was still completely buzzing as his fingers reached between us and dragged a path through the come on my abdomen. He lifted his thumb to his lips for a taste, humming like he was savoring it, then leaned down, tapping our lips and tongues together, offering me a sample.

"You like how we taste?" I murmured against his mouth.

"Mmmmmm," he moaned low in his throat, and it was so goddamn sexy.

It was even hotter when he lifted up on his elbows and then shifted his knees downward to straddle my legs. He bent forward to lick and nip at my stomach as he cleaned up our come, his mouth so sensuous that I felt gooseflesh line my legs.

When he nuzzled his nose in the hair at my groin, I felt so revered that my cock began filling again. Humming, I burrowed my fingers in his locks as he dragged his cheek against my abdomen and lightly kissed my hip bone.

Hell, this man might be the death of me.

After sliding my briefs the rest of the way down my legs, he removed his own, and deposited both on the floor. I noticed his cock had swelled again as well.

Nudging my shoulder, he rolled me on my side and slid in beside me in the sheets. We were completely naked, and he fit behind me so perfectly. He kissed my neck as his arms encircled me, and I was again engulfed in his warmth, just the way I liked.

Fuck. It was so perfect that my chest ached. I felt his breaths even out as he fell asleep with his fingertips brushing across the pulse point at my throat.

I lay awake a few minutes more until I finally succumbed as well.

---

When I woke a few hours later, I felt raw and exposed and completely sober as my eyes adjusted to the dawn hour.

I liked being in Tristan's bed way too much, but I needed things to be light between us, not as heavy as they felt in my chest.

As I carefully rolled away, he let me go, as if he knew I needed my space, even in his sleep. Damn, I loved that. It was like he understood. Understood I needed to go.

I stood and quietly pulled on my shorts and shirt before padding out to the entryway and finding my sneakers. There was a chill in the air, and I shivered against the cool morning, already dreading the ride home. I looked around, wondering if Tristan had a sweatshirt lying around somewhere that I could borrow but didn't see any.

Glancing at the bedroom door one last time, I considered climbing back in bed with that warm and sensuous and complicated man. But I was too afraid of getting sucked into something I couldn't easily escape. Tristan was all-consuming in a different way than Michael ever was, and I needed to keep a veneer between us, no matter how thin.

After I took the elevator down to the first floor and stumbled out the door to my bike, the cool air hit my skin, waking me up further. The sun was just beginning to crest on the horizon, and as I slid my leg over the seat, I knew the ride home would help clear my head.

## 21

## TRISTAN

At lunchtime, I stood at the counter and listened to a couple of my employees having a spirited discussion, across two separate rooms, about the pit bull ordinance in the city. But I was barely concentrating; my thoughts were centered on the other night with West.

Christ, that perfectly thick cock and the noises coming from his sweet lips along with the confident voice, like he'd fed right into my need to lose myself in someone.

Surprisingly enough, I didn't feel guilty about any of it. We were two consenting adults recovering from heartaches of our own, and if he wanted to be in my bed, in my arms, then I'd let him. At least for now because I needed it as much as he did. It was as if he offered me a light at the end of a long and harrowing tunnel.

"What are you all dreamy about?" Brooke asked me.

"Huh?" I replied, about to regret tuning out their conversation.

"I think he's dreaming about a certain guy in a hoodie," Elijah remarked with a smirk.

"I'll have you know he doesn't wear that hoodie anymore, not since leaving V," I replied and then immediately bemoaned admitting that out loud.

"Wait, what?" Brin asked, stopping mid-bite. "And how exactly do you know that?"

"We've become friends," I replied, rolling my eyes. "I told you that."

"Uh, yeah, *phone* friends," Brin replied. "Not in-person, no-hoodie friends."

"Details," I said, balling up the wrapper of my roast-beef sandwich. "Thing is, he's trying to make a life for himself, but he's sort of freaked by V—Michael, I mean."

"V fits him better," Brooke replied, and Brin snickered.

"When he showed up at Bent last weekend, he was...I don't know, intense."

"So nothing new." Brin rolled his eyes. "I mean, he'd drop off his dogs, and you'd think he was letting you hold the heart diamond from *Titanic* or something."

"Right?" Brooke added. "Like you were a peon he was allowing the privilege."

"Right." I sighed. "I didn't tell him that I even spoke to West. He'd try to nose his way in; he's that kind of guy, used to getting his way, if you know what I mean."

"Got it," Brooke said, and Brin agreed, but Elijah stayed strangely silent. "Well, we'd certainly never spill the beans. Not that we'd ever run into him again."

"You never know," I replied as a customer stepped inside, and both of them retreated to the doggie day-care end of the business.

Elijah was working on the grooming side with me today, and after the customer picked up her dog and left, he remained standing at the counter, staring out to the parking lot, lost in his thoughts.

"You okay?" I asked, placing my hand on his shoulder.

"Yeah," he said, shaking his head as if I'd roused him from a deep thought. "It's just... Do you think Stewart is like V?"

My stomach squeezed tight for him. He was definitely struggling, and it was obvious he needed a sounding board. "How so?"

He turned to glance at me. "Always getting his way."

I sank my elbows to the counter beside him. "*Does* he—always get his way?"

He stared out the window for a beat before answering. "One way or another, yes."

I sighed. "And what happens when you insist on something you feel strongly about?"

He rushed his fingers through his hair. "It becomes an argument, I guess."

Damn, Stewart either needed a chill pill or a wakeup call. "And how does that make you feel?"

He shook his head. "Sad and pissed off and...I don't know anymore."

"Have the arguments ever become physical?" I asked hesitantly, hoping I wasn't met with a lash of anger.

"No." He shook his head fervently. "Never."

I breathed a sigh of relief. He was obviously wrestling with his feeling on this. And being in love only muddied the waters. But love did not solve everything. Not if it wasn't right. Even Chris and I struggled with some big issues, and there were times when we felt we were growing apart, or not on the same page, but communication had fixed that.

"Want my opinion?" I asked as I straightened from the counter and glanced at the clock on the wall. We were due for two new appointments shortly.

"Please," he replied in a subdued voice.

I hoped I wouldn't regret giving him advice, especially if it only made things worse between them. But Elijah had been floundering for a while now.

"When we first met, you had this energy, you know? Vibrant and lively." I folded my arms across my chest. "And lately...I dunno; it seems like that energy has been doused."

"I hear you. I honestly don't feel like myself anymore." He looked over his shoulder as if hoping nobody heard. "What do I do?"

"I figure you've got two options. Tell him what you need, and see if he's willing to meet you halfway." I took a breath. "Or it's time to walk away. Take a break, give yourself some perspective."

His shoulders dropped as he nodded in agreement. "Thanks."

After I got busy shampooing an energetic lab-mix puppy, I refused to keep looking at my phone. I hadn't heard from West in a couple of days, but that was nothing new. Except I couldn't help wondering if we'd taken things too far and he felt like there was no going back. Maybe the easygoing texts and phone calls had been tainted, and he felt pressure from me to act a certain way now that we'd been intimate.

That was the exact reason why I wouldn't contact him first, even though I wanted to reiterate that we agreed on no strings. That would always apply, no matter what I was feeling about him. For the first time in years my mind was otherwise occupied by a certain sexy someone, and for that, I was filled with relief. Even though I felt guilt deep in my gut that I should still be grieving for Chris.

*Puh-lease*, Chris said in my head. *It's about damn time you did something just for you.*

I scratched behind the exuberant lab's ears and narrowly avoided being splashed in the face as I thrust the next thought from my head.

*Promise you'll find someone to love again. Don't be alone.*

But whatever was going on between West and me wasn't about love. It was about companionship and comfort and friendship. And scorching-hot kisses. Fuck.

After a long day, I took Mack for a walk down Edgewater, made myself a sandwich with leftover lunchmeat from my grocery store trip yesterday, and then flipped on the television, turning to a food channel, which made me smile. I recalled West telling me he'd be working the lunch shift a couple of days this week, and I hoped that meant he got to help out in the kitchen.

I anticipated possibly receiving a text from him later tonight, so when there was a knock on my condo door, I froze. My heart pattered in my chest as I looked through the peephole, fully expecting to see my neighbor or the super.

But instead it was West, awkwardly fidgeting with his hands in his pockets, so I swung open the door in a rush, wondering if something was wrong.

"Is this okay?" he asked as a flush crawled across his cheeks. "I thought if I called or texted I might chicken out, and I—"

"It's definitely okay," I replied, stepping aside so he could enter the apartment. When he walked inside and down the narrow hallway, his gaze immediately sought the window with a view of the lake as if it grounded him as much as it did me.

"It's just..." He leaned against the glass door leading to the balcony, absently petting Mack, who'd approached with his tail wagging. "I can't stop thinking about you. How you looked and smelled and *felt* the other night."

"Yeah, me too." West wanted me as much as I wanted him—that much was obvious. He was more real than my memories or fantasies. He was here in the flesh, and I could touch him if he'd let me. It was a reality that sharpened like a knife in my gut, the blade gleaming with longing but also laced with traces of anxiety, that maybe this would all fall apart somehow.

"And your mouth," West continued, gripping the metal doorjamb behind him.

I arched an eyebrow. "What about my mouth?"

"How your mouth felt on my lips, on my skin. And how it might feel on other parts of me too," he replied, fisting his length through the front of his jeans.

The need and lust in his eyes were disarming, and I sucked in a breath. "Yeah, I've thought of it too. Believe me."

As he placed his backpack on the floor our eyes met. His sparked with longing and quiet desperation. So I crowded him against the glass and took his mouth in a fiery kiss that lasted several long bone-melting moments. When he whimpered against me, I broke away, swiping at my lips, completely keyed up.

Remembering his confession from the other night and wondering if he'd been handed many opportunities, I sank to my knees in front of him before they threatened to give way from sheer yearning. It completely turned me on to imagine him using that same confident voice again, the one he used when he asked for exactly what he wanted. My need to smell him and *taste* him was overpowering.

"Fuck," West murmured, leaning his head against the window. "I...*damn*. I love how you look right now."

Lifting his shirt, he yanked it off his shoulders, and I longed to lash my tongue against his nipples, which had pebbled in anticipation.

"*Please*," he whimpered while reaching for the button on his jeans.

My hands worked to tug his jeans and underwear over his hips, and his thick cock sprang free, red-tipped and leaking. My mouth watered at the sight.

When I leaned forward to bury my nose in the patch of fine hair at his groin, I could feel him trembling. He smelled like a combination of sweat and rosemary, and I feathered kisses along the base of his shaft, savoring his scent.

His cock was silky warm in my palm as I gripped him and stroked upward. My fingertips skimmed lower to his smooth and nearly clean-shaven sac. Fuck, that was sexy.

My jaw grazed over the glistening head, and as I changed course to lick along his hip bone, his precome left a wet trail across my chin.

"This okay?" I asked, and when I glanced up at West, his irises were gleaming with undulating need.

"God, yeah." When I gave the crown a tentative lick, his fingers gripped my shoulder. His other hand fisted his dick at the thick base, and he eagerly fed it to my lips. "Need you to suck me."

His voice was gaining the same assertive edge that had me salivating the previous night. My tongue snaked out and circled the crown before licking into his slit and tasting his salty-sweet precome. "Mmmmm..."

His knees faltered as if threatening to give out, and his fingers tugged at my hair. He pumped his hips, and his thick shaft stretched my mouth to capacity as my tongue worked along one of the veins. I kept my hand low on his length, stroking in unison with the caresses of my tongue.

I could feel myself leaking inside my sweats, and I was desperate to take myself out, but it could wait. Instead, I got lost in the scent of him and the erotic noises tumbling from his throat.

I didn't know how long we stayed that way against the window, my lips and tongue bathing his cock, his fingers gripping my hair, but I was in heaven. He began thrusting in shallow stabs, expertly fucking into my mouth until I was able to take him for longer periods to the back of my throat.

When his back arched and he shuddered, I knew he was about to come. "Tristan," he groaned as his jizz coated the roof of my mouth, and I swallowed every drop he had to offer. I licked around the crown, collecting any beads I'd missed as his shaft softened and became too tender for my tongue.

I stood as he sagged against the window and pulled up his

jeans, tucking himself back in. "Fuck, that was—" he mumbled, trying to get his bearings.

My hands curving beneath his thighs, I lifted him up, and his legs wound easily around my waist. My lips fused to his, my tongue licking into his mouth, and I carried him to the couch.

# 22

# WEST

My legs encircled his waist sturdily even though the rest of me felt practically boneless as Tristan transported us to the sofa. It was so fucking sexy how he'd sunk to his knees, knowing I'd want that—need that. And how immediately after, he'd understood I'd want to be enveloped in his strong arms.

Damn, it was so perfect, and I was terrified to like it too much—how incredibly perceptive he was of me and my desires.

But I couldn't allow those thoughts to rule my brain right now. I was here because I didn't want to stay away. Not anymore. I wanted to be with him instead of going to bed alone, and he welcomed me no questions asked.

As he laid me down on the firm cushion and sank on top of me, our mouths melding together, I could feel his hard shaft digging into my stomach.

"Want your cock," I whimpered, nearly desperate for it.

When he leaned back to fish his shirt over his shoulders, my fingers stretched to fork through the soft hair on his chest, my thumbs circling his pale-brown nipples. He shivered as he pushed down his gray sweatpants, revealing his flushed length.

I licked my lips and groaned. "Take them off."

He stood up to tug his pants past his ankles before rejoining me on the couch.

"Fuck, that's nice," I admitted as his cock jutted toward his stomach. It hit me like a ton of bricks that I didn't have to hold back like I used to do with Michael. With Tristan, I was free to break out of my shell, to completely be myself and give in to exactly what I was craving, without being reminded of some set standard or rules. "Straddle me."

He groaned, his knees sinking to either side of my shoulders, and I felt the fine tremor in his thighs. He circled his length, stroked once from root to tip, and then fed me his eager cock. As I lapped at the head, he quivered, his fist digging into my hair. I loved seeing him coming apart the other night, and now I had a close-up view.

My hands, which were resting on his thighs, circled to his cheeks, and I squeezed as I took him inside my mouth. He was warm and salty, and my eyes rolled to the back of my head.

"So good," he moaned, driving his hips toward my mouth.

When my fingers traced his crease, his back bowed as he released a strangled moan.

"You like that?" I asked, licking a line across the silky skin. "For someone to play with you?"

He whimpered as his head arched to the ceiling. He was practically thrumming.

"Nice," I replied as my fingers tunneled into his crease.

When I parted his cheeks, he groaned out a curse as his cock prodded my throat, practically losing his mind.

"I can't... I won't last," he said in a strained voice.

I nodded and licked at his slit. "Want to swallow your come."

I brushed the pad of my thumb over his hole while gulping his length down again. He moaned and shuddered, hurtling over the edge. His hands gripped my hair as he spurted down my throat. I eagerly swallowed everything he offered, grateful that this beautifully complex man chose me to spend his time with, after he'd lost someone he'd shared his life with.

When he collapsed on top, I sighed against his substantial weight—somehow it grounded me. There was a smaller part of me that wondered how I measured up to Chris. But that was only fleeting. Moreover, I hoped that Tristan didn't have any regrets being with me. I wanted to make him feel good and cared for. It knocked me squarely in the chest how fucking much I wanted that. To give him what he was giving me—a chance to get his needs met, to be treasured and respected.

We rolled to our sides, so he was spooning me with scarcely any space between us as his hot breath fanned across my ear, making me shiver. "Thank you," I whispered as I burrowed farther inside his arms, and he responded with a tender peck on my cheek. The quiet and simple gesture made my stomach swoop.

For the first time, I noticed the Food Network was turned to a low hum on the television, and I eventually got lost in that night's *Chopped* episode.

At some point, I felt Tristan lifting and carrying me to his bed, so I must've fallen asleep. After he laid me down and pulled me into his arms, I heard him whisper *stay if you want* in my ear. It was the first time he'd suggested it, and somehow that sat markedly heavy in my chest.

And yet, it didn't freak me out—not this time. He curled the fingers of one hand into my hair, and with the other brushed against the pulse point in my neck. He'd done the same before, and I wasn't sure what it was about, but I was too exhausted to call attention to it.

As I settled against him, I sank into the deepest sleep, not stirring until the morning.

---

I felt a kiss on my shoulder. "You must've really been tired."

"Guess so," I replied around a yawn. "I couldn't even make my stealthy escape."

"Is that what you call it?" He smirked. "Well, you can still make it if you want. I'm jumping in the shower so I can at least get in by eight." A few minutes later, I heard him turn on the shower.

The scent of coffee wafted through the open doorway, and I suddenly had the idea of preparing a decent breakfast for him. I padded to the kitchen and searched through his cupboards, pulling out a couple of mugs as well as some eggs, milk, and cheese from the fridge.

Needing to take a leak, I walked to the bathroom. He'd left the door open a crack, so I went in and stood at the toilet. Tristan had his back to me beneath the shower, and his firm ass was on full display. Holy hot damn. I could feel myself stirring instantly.

Without thinking it through, I opened the shower stall and joined him beneath the warm spray. "This okay?" I whispered as I kissed his neck, and he hummed, twisting his head to offer me a chaste peck on the lips.

I pumped some soap into my palm and began washing his shoulders and back, taking extra time on his cheeks since I knew he'd like that, before reaching around to encircle his cock, which was fully erect from the attention.

"Put your hands on the wall for me," I murmured in his ear.

"Fuck, West," he replied with a shiver, but he did as I asked.

I peppered kisses on his shoulders before moving my lips in a line down his spine to his ass. When I sank my teeth into a meaty part of his cheek, he whimpered. I parted him open with the heels of my hands, and when I got a good look at his hole, which was a rosy shade with dark hair surrounding it, my cock lengthened in response.

"Damn, Tristan. You're gorgeous." He swore under his breath as he adjusted his palms against the tile. "Just want to get a taste."

When I leaned forward and took a swipe at his hole, he

groaned low in his throat. Opening his cheeks wider, I tenderly painted his star with my tongue. I circled the tight bud, kissing and sucking on the firm muscle, prodding it with my tongue. Succeeding in softening the skin, I pushed a finger inside.

"It's been too long since somebody—" He cursed and squirmed against me. "I'm gonna come."

Fucking him with my finger, I grasped his stiff shaft and began stroking him in unison, while nibbling at his hip bone and murmuring words of encouragement.

When he moaned my name and shot against the wall, it was the hottest fucking thing. I gently removed my digit from his pulsing hole and kissed my way up his spine to his shoulder, lightly biting it before laving it with my tongue.

He rested his forehead against the wall as he caught his breath, his shoulders sagging as my arms encircled his waist.

"Fuck, West. What the hell are you doing to me?" he groaned as my pulse spiked in my veins.

"I could ask you the same question," I replied as my hand feathered down his spine. I wanted to please him, to drive him wild, so his words lit me like a candle.

All at once he turned in my arms and took my mouth in a steamy kiss, his tongue lapping against mine. His arms reached beneath my hips, and he lifted me off the ground. In one smooth motion he spun and planted me firmly against the shower wall.

He sucked on my tongue and then attacked my neck as my cock leaked against my stomach. I loved the juxtaposition of him letting me take the lead, then in the next breath smothering me with all his warmth and weight.

"Want to taste you," he replied in a gruff voice. As soon as he released me and my legs found purchase on the tile, he slid to his knees and took the tip of my stiff cock in his mouth. His hands gripped my ass, his fingertips tunneling into my crease as he sucked me to the back of his throat.

My balls drew up tight, my groin lighting on fire as I coated his tongue in thick ropes. After he swallowed my come, he gently licked at the water around my groin as well as some precome that had pooled there. The tender action made my chest ache.

After we dried off and got dressed, Tristan poured us mugs of coffee while I cracked eggs into the frying pan.

"Did Chris cook?" I asked, having noticed more gourmet spices tucked in the back of the cupboard when I was fishing out the salt.

"Not regularly," he replied and then smirked. "We made due between the two of us *and* with takeout on regular rotation."

I smiled even though I was hit with a sudden bout of melancholy. I couldn't quite place my finger on where it'd come from, except that right then I'd pictured them sharing a meal together in their condo. Laughing. *Happy.*

"Hey," Tristan said, stepping into my space and tugging me against him. "What is it?"

"Dunno," I replied, shaking my head. "Just... Does it feel strange, being with me? You know—*sad*?"

He lifted my chin with his thumb so I was forced to meet his eyes. "No. I still have gloomy moments, probably always will...but it has nothing to do with you."

When he gently kissed me, my heart knocked against my chest.

"You make me feel alive, like the world is full of possibilities again. Being with you is amazing, exciting, *sexy*," he explained, and I grinned. "So, thank you...for giving me that."

I dipped my head, my cheeks growing warm. He kissed the top of my hair and stepped away so I could finish cooking our breakfast.

I made up two plates of scrambled eggs with cheese and a side of toast.

"Mmmm, I could get used to this," Tristan remarked as he dug into the wheat slice he'd slathered with jam.

I stiffened, not because it reminded me of Michael, who never had time in the morning for much, but because it sounded like more than *no strings attached.*

"That's not what I meant," Tristan added around a bite of food, recognizing my change in mood instantly. "That was my way of complimenting your food."

"I know," I replied in a small voice. "I enjoy cooking for you."

But something still didn't sit right with me. As he rinsed his plate in the sink, I realized exactly what it was.

I wanted him to think those things. To mean them and say them out loud.

"Take your time leaving," Tristan said, heading out the door. "Talk to you later."

*When is later?* I wanted to ask.

I didn't want him to tiptoe around me or our arrangement. Didn't want him to be so easygoing and mollifying. Not anymore. And that thought scared me most of all.

# 23

# TRISTAN

West showed up at the dock on Sunday without any formal invitation. I'd only mentioned in a text that I was going for a boat ride, and suddenly it'd become our thing. But I'd admit the line between us was beginning to blur around the edges. It was getting to the point where he was in my every thought and consideration, and if I wanted to come out of this friendship unscathed, I needed to keep a level head. Still, when he stepped onto the boat, I couldn't keep from openly grinning, the pure joy more than likely apparent on my face.

As we motored onto the water, I could feel his gaze searing into me hot and intense from his position across from me on the bench. "What?" I asked, smirking.

He arched an eyebrow. "Have you ever gone skinny-dipping in the lake?"

"On one or two occasions," I replied, trying not to recall the dream I had the other night, where West played a prominent part. "When I was younger."

I wouldn't mention it was with Chris when we couldn't keep our hands off each other. That seemed many moons ago, and yet, I felt the same thrumming in my veins now with West. But I told myself it absolutely wasn't the same thing. West and I were friends who were only fooling around, trying to temporarily meet each other's needs. With Chris, it had been so much more.

*But we were friends first*, Chris whispered on the wind. *Friends who caught on fire for each other.*

"Take yourself out so I can see you," West suggested with a devilish gleam, and I did a double-take, marveling at the contradiction. Gone was the moody, unsure kid, only to be replaced by the liberated, playful man filled with hope and mischievousness.

"What—right now?" I looked along the shoreline, and outside of a couple of faraway boats, we were virtually alone. Still, I shook my head. "I can't—"

"Sure you can," he replied with a smirk. "You look so impressive manning this boat. Distinguished, even. It would be hot to see you holding your cock while your other hand grips the wheel."

"Goddamn, West," I ground out as our eyes met briefly. "Haven't *you* come into your own... What happened to my quiet and shy companion?"

He laughed and then shrugged. "Guess he finally went after what he needed. And who he wanted."

When he curved his eyebrow in challenge, I shivered. My gaze panning the shoreline, I already knew I planned on doing precisely what he asked. Fuck, he knew exactly how to light me up and appeal to my whims—all of which seemed to include him in one fashion or another.

I jerked the throttle and reduced to a slower speed before my hand drifted to my shorts. I tugged them just far enough down that the head of my cock was exposed above the waistband as I gripped my shaft.

"Nice," he murmured in appreciation as he gazed fixedly at my dick. He stood, sidled next to me, and dragged his fingers along my shoulder blades, making the hairs on my neck stand up. Thankfully there was a glass partition that extended along the sides of the steering wheel, so unless you had a direct view, you wouldn't realize that I held my cock in my fist.

West's fingers slid beneath the waistband and into my crease.

"So hot," he whispered in my ear.

"Fuck," I groaned, arching my back.

My breathing became labored as he sank to his knees in front of me and flicked his tongue at the head of my cock. He licked at the precome as his thumb circled my hole. He tugged at my shorts until they fell to my knees, and continued his sensual assault on my shaft.

"I want to watch you lose yourself," he said, his gaze meeting mine. As he licked the underside of my crown, his thumb breached my hole. I moaned, gripping his hair in a tight fist. "I know you're close. You're so fucking sexy like this."

He was turning me inside out as he licked, then sucked me to the back of his throat. My spine tingled, my balls drew up, and my come shot out in ribbons across his tongue. His eyes remained glued to mine the whole time he swallowed my jizz, and I tried hard to stay upright and not steer off course.

"Fuck, you're amazing," I said as he kissed my softened shaft and then helped lift my shorts to their proper place on my hips.

"The feeling's mutual," he murmured in my ear before offering me a peck on the cheek. "Go skinny-dipping with me?"

I arched an eyebrow. "You want me to set anchor?"

He nodded. "But you still have to hold me and make sure I don't drown."

My heart squeezed at the vulnerability in his words when just moments before he was a hot and sexy devil licking me into submission.

"Of course," I replied, trying to rein in my breaths as well as my pulse so I could find a decent place to drop anchor. In another minute, my legs wouldn't feel as rubbery as they did now. "Wasn't sure if you were interested in going back in."

"Only if you're with me," he replied, and his gaze held mine for a long beat.

I felt a winging in my chest. *Damn.*

"Thanks for putting your trust in me," I replied around a parched throat as I steered farther from the shore. "Let's do this."

I chose a spot to drop anchor in the middle of Lake Erie, and as soon as it felt secure enough, I pushed my shorts down and jumped in the refreshing water before I chickened out. Besides, I could've used some cooling off right then.

Going under completely nude felt so free and uninhibited, I whooped in sheer joy as I broke the surface. West chuckled as he walked to the edge of the boat. He looked left, then right, before yanking his shorts down and kicking out of them. He was sporting a semi, and I sucked in a breath, seeing that gorgeous cock lying across his thigh. He was obviously turned on by the experience or by what we'd done on the boat.

Facing toward the front of the bow with his pretty ass on full display, he cautiously lowered himself into the water, holding on to the platform for leverage. I swam up behind him and hissed against his neck as my cock bumped his ass. "You're going to make it hard to concentrate."

"Try your best," he said with a smirk as he shivered.

"You can let go. I've got you." He detached his fingers from the plank instantly. His blind faith made my breath hitch.

We practiced floating for a while, which caused his shaft to break the surface of the water at different points, and I had the urge to lick him from head to toe.

"Stop looking at my cock," he chided as he sank down in the water again. "You're making me so fucking hard."

"I can't help it; it's gorgeous. *You're* gorgeous," I murmured, my cheeks firing up. "I'm sure you've been told that before."

He shook his head. "Not like that. Everything with you is so much more—"

He looked away and took a deep breath.

"More what?" I said into his neck as my hand clutched at his waist.

"Dunno, maybe...important is the word. *Special*."

I lifted his chin with my thumb, forcing him to look at me. I needed him to be honest with me. "Is that a bad thing?"

"No, it's not," he replied, sighing. "But it's hard to think of you the same way I'd think of a hookup."

I nodded in agreement. "Maybe because we're also friends."

"I'd hate to lose your friendship over us...fucking around." He shrugged.

"Yeah...yeah, me too," I admitted. "Just means we have to agree to communicate better if..."

"If what?" he asked as he used his arms to propel himself in the water just like I'd taught him.

"If things get to be too much...or *strange*."

After he tried swimming by himself using the breaststroke I'd demonstrated, he held on to my back for a while and we swam together. Having him right up against me like that was almost too much. But it was also everything. It felt like we were molded together, and somehow it made me feel closer to him, not only physically but also emotionally.

I twisted around to face him, and we made out for a while, rubbing our hands freely over each other's wet skin beneath the surface. We were both rock solid in the water, completely turned on.

All at once we heard a motor in the distance as a couple of boats cruised toward us, and eventually we had to let go of our intimate embrace, especially when one of them anchored nearby.

We snuck back onto the boat and into our clothes, hoping to remain undetected by the strangers. I pulled anchor, and we sped away, sharing secret smiles between us.

When we got back to the dock, it was way more crowded than a couple of hours prior, and I remembered there was a music festival happening at Whiskey Island tonight. We left his bike chained to the post and walked around, listening to folk and rock music for a bit before sitting down at two spots that'd been vacated at the tiki bar. As we ordered beers and burgers, West continued looking around as if he'd spot Michael in the crowd, and I wished he could finally feel more relaxed about the situation.

It was odd, and yet strangely, I got it. Like the fear of constantly running into your ex after a terrible breakup. But he and Michael had more baggage than that—an entire history that included Michael being a sort of caretaker to him. Pretty messed up.

"It's Labor Day next weekend," I pointed out, and West nodded as he sipped his beer. "I'll be out of town on Thursday and Friday."

He stopped mid-swallow. "Where to?"

"Chris's family owns a house in Port Clinton, and every year we head there for a couple of days," I explained. The whole area was filled with small islands, some of them quaint and picturesque.

"And you still keep up the tradition?" he asked, his eyebrows drawing together.

"Yeah, I do," I replied after chewing on a fry. "Plus, Mack loves it there too."

It might've been a strange concept to some, but as I'd already explained, over the years they'd become my family.

West looked sort of a cross between bummed and freaked out, and I pondered if it was because I was leaving or because I had a family to spend holidays with. The thought weighed wearily on me. I'd have been in the same situation as West if Chris's mother and sister hadn't welcomed me into their lives so early on. Michael might've been considered more like family to West if there wasn't the muddled part about them hooking up.

I set my beer down and angled my head toward him. "So I wondered if—"

"No way," he replied, his hands flying up. "Besides, I have to work."

When I chuckled, he looked perplexed.

"I wasn't going to ask you to come to Port Clinton," I pronounced, and his face dropped, embarrassment coloring his cheeks. "Not that it wouldn't be fun...*sometime*."

"Or awkward," he mumbled, and I smirked. *Definitely*.

"I was actually going to ask if you'd come see the air show from the boat on Sunday," I explained, motioning toward the docks.

"Oh." His eyes widened as his gaze scanned the water. "It's *that* cool?"

"To have planes flying directly over your head?" I replied with a cocked eyebrow. "Hell yeah. We stay docked because fighting for a spot out on the water is a hassle. But it doesn't matter where you are as long as you're this close to Burke Lakefront Airport. It's *amazing*."

His gaze darted to the sky as if imagining it. "Who else will be there?"

"My friends from work." I shrugged. "Maybe Chris's family."

He stiffened for a brief moment and then bit his lip as if formulating an excuse.

"I get it; it's strange being around all new people," I remarked, thumping his knee.

"Or many people at all," he supplied, and my fist clenched, thinking about just how sheltered he'd felt this whole time.

"You've technically already met Chris's mom and sister," I continued.

"And at some point, you've got to ask yourself if you're living for you or just hiding from *him*."

He stared at me with wide eyes as if he hadn't even considered that fact. Michael had drained a good chunk of time and experience from him; he shouldn't deplete any more.

"Whatever you decide," I said around a sip of beer, "I respect your choice. I just wanted to make the offer. It's been three years since I last made the effort to even show down here, and…I'm trying to live again too."

He nodded as he kept his gaze leveled on mine.

"You've…really helped with that, you know?" I said in a hesitant voice.

"What do you mean?" he asked, and I could see his pulse pounding at his throat.

"You've drawn me out of my shell. My *grief*. Showed me it's time to start enjoying things again."

His jaw dropped open. "I have?"

"You have," I replied with a small smile. "So…thank you."

"I have stuff to thank you for too," he said suddenly.

I pushed my plate away and leaned closer to hear him better as the tempo of the music increased. "Like what?"

"Letting me put my trust in you," he murmured close to my ear, his hand landing on my knee, sending a shockwave through my system. "Showing me there are solid and decent people in the world. Being a friend but not hovering…and instead, letting me spread my wings."

*Damn.* My fingers grazed against his as he held my gaze, his eyes softening, and I had the urge to kiss him right there out in the open.

"It's not a hardship, and seeing the change in you has been nothing short of incredible," I replied around a parched throat. "I think…we're probably still scared, though. Of different things. But yet kind of similar too."

"Yeah?" he asked, glancing down at our intertwined fingers.

"We're both afraid of losing again," I replied as my thumb traced over his palm, making him shiver. "Losing people we cherish, losing *ourselves*. Facing those things."

"True," he whispered. I felt him absently twirling my wedding band around my finger, and my breath hitched. When my gaze followed the motion, he asked, “Do you think you’ll always wear this in Chris’s memory?”

A large boulder formed in my throat just thinking about ever getting rid of it or even losing it. “Dunno. Do you think it would bother somebody? Somebody I might date...in the future.”

His eyes met mine, and it was as if the music faded away and it was just him and me in our own little perfect bubble. “Depends, I guess.”

“On what?” I asked, my pulse pounding in my ears.

“On what the new guy means to you,” he said as his fingers traced up my wrist, creating gooseflesh in their wake. “Or whether or not he hopes to give you something equally special one day.”

“Yeah,” I responded, drawing back, my heart clogging with emotion. Fucking hell, this man was so adorable, my chest ached.

Looking for a change in subject, I chugged back my beer, the mood a bit sobering. Once he did the same, I turned in my seat. “How about you let me drive you home this time?”

Without a moment’s hesitation, he nodded. We left a tip, walked to the parking lot, and loaded his bike in the back of my truck. As I drove him to Ohio City, he pointed out the Italian restaurant where he worked and then let me drop him off directly in front of the house he rented.

“West...um, thanks,” I said as he reached for the door handle, not wanting to directly spell out the fact that he’d trusted me again.

When he turned to me, his eyes were filled as much with affection as with trepidation. All I could think to do was reach for him and pull him into a deep and melting kiss that left me rock solid and longing for him all the way home.

## 24

# WEST

As I biked closer to the docks, Edgewater Beach as well as Whiskey Island were packed to the gills with people watching the afternoon air show. Due to limited parking, the road to the slips was blocked from entry, so I wouldn't have been able to get near the boats with a car even if I owned one. Not at this late hour.

Was I really doing this? I almost asked Marco if he wanted to join me, just to have backup. But truth be told, I was dying to see Tristan. I hadn't been this compelled to be around somebody since the first boy I fell for in high school. And this was exactly how it felt, like some feverish crush on an older, beautiful man. *Christ.*

Getting through the crowd was daunting. I had to climb off my bike and carefully wind around groups of people on blankets with coolers of beer and wine and food, simply enjoying the nice weather and the music blaring from the tiki bar area.

This week had felt strange without Tristan around, which was a ridiculous thought since it was only about a ninety-minute drive to Port Clinton and we mostly texted anyway. Still, he sort of sounded distant in his responses. I didn't know if it was because he was with his late husband's family, and maybe being there had conjured up plenty of memories for him.

I understood all too well how memories could wreck you. As a teen, I'd once taken a bus back to my family's home in Old Brooklyn just to be on the street where I grew up. Except the house had been demolished, and not having anything at all to look at besides a large empty lot made me feel just as vacant. I vaguely remembered Serena mentioning the first responders retrieving some things from the fire, but other than the necklace I wore, which had been presented to me by the social worker on her final home visit before closing the case, Serena never brought it up again.

I'd shared that memory with Tristan one of the times we'd talked on the phone late into the night, and I remembered how his voice changed to soft and comforting. I couldn't talk about that stuff with Michael, or anyone else for that matter, except maybe the therapist the county assigned me at the time. But I was pretty angry and distraught back then. Michael was a self-made businessman just like his own father—whom I'd overheard Serena call a bastard once—and he couldn't be bothered with anybody else's sob stories. *Suck it up,* he'd said once when he'd heard me punching the hell out of my pillow as a teen, even though I was doing the exact thing the counselor had told me to do when I was feeling emotional.

The moment I neared Slip 23, my throat clogged up on me. The boat was packed with people, but all I could see was Tristan. With his chestnut-brown hair, cutoff shorts, and tight T-shirt. His eyes lit up as soon as he noticed me in the crowd, and it made my heart pound a steady beat in my chest.

I chained my bike up to the usual post, and Tristan met me on the dock.

"So glad you made it," he said, gripping my shoulder.

"Yeah, me too," I replied and then motioned to the grass area. "But it's a zoo down here."

"It always is," he acknowledged, looking me over from my hair down to my sneakers and then upward again, landing pointedly on my mouth.

"I won't kiss you in front of all these people," he whispered, making the butterflies in my stomach beat their wings wildly. "But I hope to get a chance later."

I swallowed roughly. "Me too."

"Let me introduce you to some people," he said as his fingers scaled down my arm and casually brushed against mine. I followed him to the boat and stepped inside after him.

"You already know Brin, and that's his boyfriend, Nick." The two attractive guys, one blond, one brunet, were sitting closely together, their arms entwined.

"Nice to see you again, West," Brin replied, and his boyfriend lifted his beer in greeting and smiled in my direction.

"And this is Brooke," Tristan announced, playfully nudging the woman I recognized from the grooming business. "Her husband, John, and their two kids."

The two boys had lines cast over the side of the boat as their dad instructed them to refrain from shaking the poles and scaring off the fish. But it fell on deaf ears. Brooke rolled her eyes and raised her hand in a wave.

"You've met Sheri and Judy," Tristan said as we turned to the other side of the boat. *Chris's family.* They sat side by side, red Solo cups and a bottle of wine between them on the seat. My pulse pounded in my ears.

"How was the ride over?" Sheri asked, glancing at the dock.

"Congested," I replied, feeling uneasy, especially since she'd eyed Tristan's bike last time I met them. "But at least I could maneuver through the crowd."

"Which direction did you come from?" Judy asked innocently enough, but I

bristled anyway. They were only being polite with their

inquiry, like they'd be with any stranger. I logically knew I needed to stop hiding. It'd been months since I left Michael.

"Ohio City. So not that far away."

As if Tristan sensed the questions would be too much for me, he placed his hand on the small of my back and steered me toward the front of the ship. "Let me introduce you to a couple of other friends."

I followed him as he stepped up on the bow first and led me toward two men sitting there, one of whom I recognized from his business. "This is Elijah and his friend Kam. Kam owns the Spin Cycle bike shop." And as his fingers brushed against my waist, I knew it was meant to be an inside joke between us.

"This is probably the best spot to watch the show. Let me get you a beer," Tristan said as he retreated to the main-cabin area again.

Once I sank down in an open space beside Elijah, I felt like I could breathe again, and I had a sneaking suspicion Tristan knew that'd be the case. Up here I'd be safe from more prying eyes and probing questions.

"How's the bike holding up?" Kam asked with a hint of humor in his eyes. He was a very attractive Asian man, and from his casual demeanor, he didn't seem to think my having Tristan's bike was a big thing. Though I was more than curious what Tristan had shared with this group about our friendship and how it had developed under unusual circumstances.

"Eh, I've ridden better," I deadpanned, and he chuckled. "Just kidding. It's actually really sturdy."

"If you ever need any adjustments, just bring it up to the shop," he said, and it was such a kind offer that my shoulders unwound further.

"It's nice that you came," Elijah remarked. He appeared sort of melancholy, and if the dark circles beneath his eyes were any indication, he'd had a rough night. "Tristan has been *West this* and *West that* for months."

When I sucked in a breath, he nudged my knee and chuckled.

"Just messing with you," he replied. "But we can all tell he's smitten with you, and we're glad because he's had a tough road."

My heart beat unsteadily as I nodded, unable to think of anything to say in response that wouldn't incriminate me. The fact that he thought Tristan was as enamored with me as I was with him made me pause. Were we in too far over our heads?

*No strings attached*, I reminded myself.

Why did it feel like we were already uncannily tethered by some sort of thick line?

*Maybe we're supposed to be in each other's lives for a reason.*

"And I know you've had a rough time of it too," Elijah added. "Breakups *suck*."

The way he said it, I could tell he was likewise talking about himself. Did he also have some recent heartache? I searched through my brain for the late-night conversations I had with Tristan about his work friends. He *had* mentioned Brin's and Elijah's boyfriends.

"All you need is time and perspective," Kam supplied. "But yeah, it can suck."

I felt the tension inside me dissolve. Turned out everybody went through shit and were just trying to get through life. This was a perfect reminder, and I had to wonder if Tristan leaving me here with the excuse of getting me a drink had been intentional.

"What sucks most right now is to be around ridiculously happy couples," Elijah said, shooting a look over his shoulder in Brin and Nick's direction. "Except some people really have it coming, and Tristan is one of them."

"Damn straight," Kam said. "Speaking of happy couples, when is Nick moving out?"

"End of the month," Elijah responded, and I remembered Tristan mentioning that Elijah and Nick were roommates. "Hey, need a new place to stay? I've got a room for rent."

The idea of being back on this side of town was appealing but would leave me too exposed to run-ins with Michael. Besides, I couldn't even afford real wheels to get me to and from work. Not yet.

Suddenly there was a roar of engines approaching from the east side of the marina, and everybody's eyes darted to the sky. "The show's about to start," Chris's mom remarked from behind me.

A moment later, Tristan returned with a beer and handed it to me. "You good?"

"Absolutely," I replied as he sat down beside me, and I could feel the heat from his arm as it brushed against mine. That, along with the first sighting of the Blue Angels flying in dramatic fashion, made me shiver.

Damn, Tristan had been right. Watching the planes streaking directly overhead in various mind-bending maneuvers was completely breathtaking. They felt so close that the hairs stood up on the back of my neck.

When Tristan's fingertips grazed mine, raw need echoed inside me, a loud and resounding buzzing in my chest. I wanted him to pull me on his lap and wrap me tightly in his arms. To feel his breath against my neck, his mouth against my skin, his voice against my ear. When it came to the gorgeous man sitting beside me, everything felt settled on its axis again. Like he was the gravity holding me to this very earth, keeping me not only safe and protected, but grounded.

"What do you think?" he whispered in my ear near the finale, where the planes formed a seemingly perfect line and roared by us in flawless formation.

"Incredible," I replied and met his gaze. "Thanks for inviting me." His eyes softened.

Beside us, Elijah shifted to his knees to take a final photo with his phone.

About an hour later, as we were vacating the boat, Chris's mom and sister were behind me on the dock as I unchained my bike from the post. I was avoiding eye contact because I honestly didn't know what they thought of my friendship with Tristan.

"It was nice to see you again," Sheri said, and I glanced up at her in surprise.

"Thanks, you too," I replied, and just as I was forming some remark or other about the air show, she exclaimed, "Tristan likes you."

"I like him too," I remarked without hesitation. But I didn't know how that would go over, so I winced and blurted out my next thoughts. "I'm sorry."

"Don't be," Judy said. "He's the best kind of person, and you make him smile."

My pulse pounded in my throat even as a small grin lined my lips.

"He makes you smile too," Judy added with a wink.

"He does," I replied, feeling equal parts guilty and conflicted. "But I'm not—"

"No," Judy said, holding up her hand. "Please don't think you have to explain anything to us."

"It's just... We see that light in his eyes again, and it reminds us—" Sheri attempted to explain as she cleared her throat.

"A long time ago, there were two boys who became good friends and did everything together," Judy said as her eyes filled with unshed tears, and I felt mine stinging in response. "They were such a good fit that eventually they fell in love and shared a beautiful life together."

Sheri's arm wrapped around her mom's shoulder, and she kissed her cheek affectionately. "What we're saying is, there's nothing wrong with just being friends—being a comfort to each other. I hope you don't mind that Tristan told us you've had some hard things happen in your life as well."

"He sort of couldn't help it," Judy added. "He was stuck with us, and we put him on the spot."

They laughed wholeheartedly, and I couldn't help grinning in response.

"I've got a lot to figure out in my life," I said around a tight throat, not understanding why I was suddenly opening up to these women. But damn, they were so authentic, and their grief mirrored my own in so many ways. "I'm not sure I'm worthy of someone like Tristan."

"Don't ever sell yourself short," Judy said, patting my hand, and it was such a motherly thing to say that my chest squeezed tight. "Hopefully we'll see you again soon."

"Tristan tells us you're a good cook," Sheri added. "For Christ's sake, at least help the man out, give him some basic skills."

"Hey, I heard that," Tristan pronounced as he returned from walking his friends to the grassy area near the parking lot.

They laughed as each kissed him on the cheek in turn.

As we followed them along the footpath, Tristan whispered, "Sorry if they put you on the spot. I'm almost afraid to ask—"

"No, it's okay—they were actually really cool." Holy fuck, my brain was having trouble even processing their gracious words. They were good people who cared a hell of a lot for the man walking beside me. I wouldn't want him to get hurt any more than they did, and that thought rested heavily in my gut.

As Tristan momentarily squeezed my hand, his wedding band prodding my palm, I felt the earth tilting on its axis again.

# 25

# TRISTAN

As soon as the door to my condo shut, I pushed West against the wall and sucked on his lips, my hands tunneling beneath his shirt to his warm flesh. I felt like I'd been starving for a taste of him for weeks instead of days. His very presence reawakened something inside me—that fragile thing fluttering its damaged wings, longing to take flight and finally soar.

"I need this fucking mouth, Tristan," West begged in a strained voice as my thumbs traced over his nipples and they pebbled at my touch. "Want you on your knees."

I offered him one more blistering kiss, my mouth sucking on the tip of his tongue before I drew back and led him to the bedroom, both of us shedding our clothing as we went. Stumbling our way around Mack with his wagging tail and eager eyes, I paused only to acknowledge him with a *good boy* before fusing our mouths back together—hands gripping, teeth clashing, tongues lashing, like we needed to devour each other.

After I nudged him to sit down on the bed, I positioned myself on my knees in front of his spread legs and fully erect shaft. Just the sight of his thick cock with its glistening head, his sac hanging low and heavy, made my breath catch.

"Suck me," he said in a commanding voice as his thumb tilted my chin up. There was affection in his gaze but also a hunger bordering on desperation that probably mirrored my own.

I fucking loved being more submissive during sex, and the fact that West got off on being dominant really checked some boxes for me. Chris and I were both vers, which worked well for us, but something about West's needy eyes and voice stirred something entirely different inside me. I was responsible for so many other things in my everyday life, so being told what to do in the bedroom by a sexy man? I got off on it big-time.

I grabbed the base of West's cock and lowered my mouth to nuzzle each of his balls; the smell of rosemary mixed with sweat had my senses singing, and feeling the scratch of dark pubes that he kept neatly trimmed made me greedy. Holy hell.

Lifting my head, I swirled my tongue around the crown before licking up and down the length, imagining what his thick shaft might feel like inside me.

I realized how much I wanted it—fuck, did I want it—my hole clenching just thinking about that mushroom head stretching me wide, the burn grounding me.

*Forgive me, Chris.*

*You're allowed to be happy. Please don't be alone.*

I looked up at West's blissed-out eyes, then his lips, wet from my earlier kisses, before I suckled his tip; the head stretched my lips as I inched him to the back of my throat. A choked moan released from him as he grabbed at my shoulders, digging his nails in and then moving up to my hair, pulling, making my scalp sting.

My cock was hard and leaking, straining toward my stomach, and I wasn't sure how much longer I would last. If I even touched myself right now, I might detonate. Instead, I focused on worshipping the enticing cock in front of me, taking my time as I mapped the entire length with rousing flicks of my tongue.

I was rewarded with shuddery breaths and my name falling

from his lips in a reverent whisper, which only enhanced the experience of bringing him pleasure and fulfilling a need inside me at the same time.

His fingers skimmed beneath my chin. "I haven't been able to think of much else this week."

I moaned and continued licking him, my eyes rolling in the back of my head. His hands plastered on the bed, he arched his back. "So goddamn good."

I kissed the end of his cock, collecting the precome on my tongue.

"West, I...I *want* you," I confessed in a shy voice. "Want you to fuck me."

"Holy hell," he moaned as he clenched the base of his cock to stave off his orgasm. I drew away, wiping my mouth and waiting for his response while I got my unsteady pulse under control.

"Are you s-sure?" he asked. Our eyes met and held, our mouths breathing the same air, as something significant passed between us. The molecules swirling around us became thicker, not only mixed with an achingly tender longing but with emotions that suddenly surfaced and were exposed in his gaze, in his soft fingers landing on my chin, in his raw demand a moment later. "I want that too. So damn much."

I reached in the nightstand drawer for the bottle of lube I used to jerk off with, but then glanced at West, realizing I wouldn't have a condom. Chris and I hadn't had to use them in years. Realization dawned on his face, and he bent down to reach for his shorts, fishing one out of his wallet.

Satisfied we were all set, I felt my entire body light up in anticipation as I positioned myself on my hands and knees on the bed. Holy fuck, this was really happening.

I'd been this vulnerable to him in the shower the other morning, but this felt different, weightier. I was giving myself to him—this person who challenged me as much as he enchanted me—even though I had no idea where we'd end up two weeks from now. For all I knew, West could disappear into a crowd and I'd never see him again. I swallowed thickly, accepting the odds, just wanting him to take me, make me his for one mesmerizing night.

West circled the bed, his fingers brushing up and down my spine and over the globes of my ass, prodding my thighs farther apart. "You're so gorgeous, Tristan. So fucking perfect."

I made a noise in the back of my throat that made West's eyes snap to mine. They softened right before he inhaled sharply through his nose. These past couple of weeks had turned into something more, and we both knew it.

We hadn't named it out loud, but with each encounter—each text, look, touch, and kiss—it had changed the foundation of who we'd become to each other. I was falling for this broken boy turned stunning man, and I was so fucking afraid to even admit it to myself.

Tonight could leave him overwhelmed or running scared, but I was still willing to see it through because I wanted it—wanted *him*—so fucking bad—even if I was the one who ended up hurt. Opening myself up like this wasn't something I had anticipated doing, but there was just something about West that I needed. Like a visceral ache in my chest.

Even from that first night.

"Tell me again you want this," he said as he knelt beside me on the bed, tore open the condom, and rolled it down his cock.

"Please," I whimpered, growing impatient, my cock leaking against the sheets. "I want to feel you inside me."

West swore under his breath as he grabbed the lube, squirted some on his fingers, and slid them up and down his cock. He reached forward and finally...finally circled my hole with his thumb. I made a noise, half sigh, half moan.

When he pushed a digit in I hissed, finally feeling that fullness I'd been missing, craving, for years. He fucked me with his finger, murmuring how pretty my hole was while I clenched around him, and then he pushed another digit inside.

My back arched and my jaw clamped because my sac was full and begging for release and we hadn't even gotten to the fucking yet.

"Think you're ready to take my cock?"

I knew it would burn; it'd been a while, but it was time, and fuck, I was so ready. I reached my arms back, grabbed my cheeks, and pulled them open for him.

"Goddamn, Tristan," he rasped, and before I knew it, his cock was pushing at my entrance.

It stung like a motherfucker, but I also welcomed the pain; it somehow centered me. Always had. When he prodded past the rim, his fingers pressed into my shoulders, pausing. "You okay?" he ground out, sounding like he was having an equally hard time.

Soon the pain transformed into pleasure, and my eyes rolled back. Damn, I missed this. Being stretched so wide by a cock. "Holy fuck, that's—"

I felt flayed wide open as he worked his shaft inside me inch by glorious inch. Goddamn, it felt so good—too good. West's fingers dug into my thighs hard enough to leave marks. When he was buried to the hilt he leaned forward, connecting his chest to my back, and kissed tenderly along my neckline. I could feel his silver chain dragging over my shoulder blades, adding a cooling sensation to my skin. "S'good. I fucking love being inside you."

"Want to feel you," I begged, pushing my hips against his groin and feeling his sac full and heavy against the back of my thighs. "Really feel you."

West straightened and pulled almost all the way out before slamming forward again, providing the perfect rhythm and friction. He began swiveling his hips, coming at me from a different angle and hitting my prostate just right. "Uhhggggg..."

His arm slung around my chest, and he lifted me upward so we were connected again. He took my mouth in a fierce kiss, our tongues tangling together at an awkward angle, before he grabbed hold of my cock and stroked me root to tip.

I moaned as I rocked toward him, my brain short-circuiting; the only laser focus was on the sensations going on in my body. My crazy pulse, my tight chest and groin, the electric heat traveling up my spine.

"Fuck, Tristan. I need... I want..." Suddenly West pulled out, and I protested with a whine before realizing that he was positioning himself to lie beneath me.

He gripped my hips and nudged me forward so that I straddled him.

"Ride me," he growled. "I want to see you."

I wasted no time aligning his cock with my hole and stuffing him back inside.

"Fuck," he ground out as his fingernails dug into my hips. "So sexy."

At this angle I felt his thick shaft deeper, making me sway and moan, my cock leaking against my stomach. I began swiveling my thighs as he clutched onto my hips, his teeth clenched together, sweat pooling at his temples. "West, fuck. You feel so good."

My entire body thrummed as I felt that familiar pull at my groin, my balls filling and lifting up at a rapid pace as I groaned out his name and shot all over his stomach.

He moaned, gripped my hips tighter, and thrust upward through my orgasm, finally shuddering and pumping his load inside me. "So fucking incredible."

As we caught our breath, our eyes remained glued to each other, our fingers entwined, and I felt the first sting of tears. I closed my eyes and swallowed them down.

As if sensing how emotionally raw I felt in that moment, he immediately reached for me. I sank forward, my mouth meeting his in a deep and overwhelming kiss that melted me from the inside. He sucked on my lips and stroked my hair, murmuring my name in an awed tone.

Drawing away, I kissed his jaw and down his throat to his

chest, licking all the come I could reach, even around the base of his cock; he was sporting a semi again.

"You're amazing," he hummed as I collapsed on top of him again and let him taste my come, my tongue licking deeply into his mouth. His fingers dug into my hair as he held my lips directly against his, and his eyes softened as he marveled at me.

"Thank you," he whispered against my mouth.

"Thank *you*," I whispered back, and then we grinned at each other.

Pecking his cheek, I rolled off the bed. I made sure Mack was fed and had enough water as West threw away the condom, used the restroom, and straightened the sheets. I took Mack outside and let him waddle along the grass in front of the condo for a few minutes before finally slipping back into bed, and pulling West against my chest. I completely enveloped him in my arms as he sighed and melted into my frame, transforming once again into the West that needed to be held and comforted.

As he dozed off, I couldn't stop wondering at the man in my arms—his long, fluttering eyelashes, the five o'clock shadow forming on his jaw, his lean, toned torso and arms. That pretty cock lying softly on his groin.

Not one shred of guilt could make its way inside about letting him fuck me tonight. No regrets, no matter what happened between us going forward. For the first time in three years, maybe four, I'd done something completely for myself—for my own raw and unfiltered joy. In sweet and blissful surrender.

Maybe someday in the weeks ahead, if West disappeared again to take hold of his own life, the visceral memory of our night together would wither away to allow doubt and disappointment to take center stage. But at this very moment, with West in my arms, his lips at my throat, it was like catching a glimpse of a rare shooting star in all its blazing and dreamlike wonder.

As I pulled the sheets over us and hunkered down to sleep, my fingers found his pulse point, which was steady and strong, and I heard Chris's voice in my head. A voice that had grown quieter in days past.

*Don't worry, I'm still here. Always will be.*

And for the first time, it didn't make me ache with sorrow. Instead, it filled me with a glittery array of light and hope.

## 26

# WEST

THE FOLLOWING MORNING BOTH OF OUR WORKPLACES WERE CLOSED for Labor Day. I squinted my eyes open just past dawn, and my heart thrummed in my chest when I felt Tristan's heat behind me.

So many damn things were rushing through my mind—and not one of them revolved around leaving Tristan's arms. Unlike so many times before, when I'd taken off.

"You're still here." His voice was hoarse against my ear as he shifted his legs.

I entwined my fingers with his and settled back against him. "Not going anywhere."

After we finally roused, I made us some egg-and-cheese omelets, and he acted like every bite he took was a delicacy. It only made me want to cook every meal for him. We walked Mack along the back of the property, and it felt good to simply be together and not question our intentions. The night before had been intense, holy fucking hot, and so emotionally tender that no words could properly describe how I was feeling in that moment.

Feeling lazy, we napped a little more on his couch, spooned together with a movie playing in the background, but by late afternoon, we decided to lounge by the pool. Tristan lent me some swim trunks, then grabbed two beach towels from his linen closet, and we headed downstairs.

Given that Labor Day was technically viewed as the last day of summer, I was surprised there were only a handful of people swimming in the pool or soaking up the sun on lawn chairs. The rest of September would be blazing hot, but according to a sign affixed to the gate when we entered, the pool would close for the season by next weekend.

"Want to practice swimming?" Tristan asked from his lounge chair after we'd slathered sunscreen on our skin. "At least you can touch the bottom in certain parts."

I took a deep breath and stood up. "Sounds good."

We entered the pool from the shallow end and slowly made our way past three splashing kids as we got used to the temperature of the water. We practiced floating as well as the breaststroke in the five-foot section with Tristan supporting me and then letting go. I had definitely come a long way from that first time off the boat.

At one point the three kids stopped what they were doing and found my inability to swim way more entertaining.

"Hey, mister," the little blonde girl called over to me. "Want to borrow my arm floaties?"

That got a laugh from almost everyone seated close to our side of the pool, including the girl's parents.

"I'll let you know," I replied with a sheepish grin. "But hopefully after today I'll be able to manage all by myself."

Tristan squeezed my hand beneath the water and grinned at me, making my heart flutter in my chest. We worked at it for the better part of an hour, until it dissolved in a dunking and splashing match between us.

---

STEPPING INTO THE WARM SHOWER FELT SOOTHING AS WE WASHED the chlorine from our skin and made out beneath the spray.

Then we walked Mack down Clifton to the only store open, and they waited outside while I loaded a basket with a box of penne pasta and a couple of cans of whole tomatoes from the grocery section so I could whip up a simple dinner using additional ingredients from his pantry.

On the way to the register, I threw in a packet of condoms, hoping it wasn't too presumptuous of me, but when I let him peek inside the bag on the way back, he grinned. "Good idea."

We had dinner on his balcony under the setting sun, and it felt special to simply hang with Tristan. I could see in his eyes that the feeling was mutual. He seemed relaxed and pleased having me here.

After we loaded his dishwasher, he said, "Anytime you want to leave, just say the word, and I can drive you home. I don't want you to feel—"

"I don't," I replied before he could ruin it by using the words *obligated* or *awkward*. "This is one of the best days I've had in a long time."

His breath hitched as our eyes met. "Me too," he whispered as he struggled to swallow. I had to glance elsewhere before I felt too bogged down with emotion again.

Despite our nap, we retired to bed early, both wiped from the sun and the busy weekend. When he enclosed me in his warm arms, I felt so damn content, I never wanted him to let me go.

When I stirred in the middle of the night, I realized we had somehow changed positions. Tristan was lying on his stomach with the pillow pulled over his head, and I wondered if this was how he normally slept when alone in bed.

My chest was plastered to his back, and my face was in the crook of his neck. He was so warm and relaxed, I was tempted to taste his skin, so I brushed my lips against his nape, which made him shiver, even in his sleep.

In another few seconds, his hips squirmed beneath me, telling me he was awake and more than likely aroused, so I ground my lengthening cock into the crease of his ass.

His arm reached back to hold my thigh in place as he thrust upward, telling me all I needed to know. I tugged his underwear over his thighs and nipped at the meatiest part of his butt cheek. He groaned into the mattress as I fumbled for the condom and lube from the nightstand.

The room was silent except for the rustling sheets and the sound of our heavy breathing, which only made my cock grow stiffer as I rolled on the condom and clumsily slathered on some lube.

Straddling Tristan, I pressed against his shoulder with the palm of my hand as I pushed my cock inside his tight hole. I paused, allowing the sensation of being inside him to wash over me. He was hot and soft and inviting all at the same time.

His breaths were shuddery as his fingers gripped the pillow, and I ground into him in slow, measured circles, hitting his prostate.

My panting turned harsh as my pulse pounded in my ears. Tristan's moans pierced the stillness of the night as he ground his cock into the mattress for friction.

He groaned through his orgasm as I collapsed onto his back, shuddering through my own. Treasuring this connection with him, I remained still as my cock softened. My lips grazed his shoulder, and his arms reached back for my hands, knotting our fingers together and bringing them to rest above his head.

"Fuck, Tristan," I whispered in his ear. "I love being inside you."

My heart was battering against his back, and I heard him sigh into his pillow.

"Me too," he replied in a throaty voice.

I could feel his wedding band digging into my skin, and for

the first time I wondered if there would ever be a man special enough to make him consider removing it.

I felt instantly guilty for even having the thought.

By the time I pulled out and reached for a discarded T-shirt to clean us both up, Tristan had already drifted back to sleep, so I just cast the condom in the trash and slipped back inside his warmth.

## 27

# TRISTAN

The manager pulled me aside today, West had texted last night.

**About the server position?**

**No,** he explained. **He told me that Cook Tony recommended me to Chef Leanne in their new Westlake location. As a kitchen assistant or porter.**

My heart leapt in excitement for him. **That's amazing.**

**Yeah, it's pretty cool.** A long pause. **Except Westlake is pretty far to travel.**

I struggled with how to respond. He was right. He only had a bike, and Westlake was a good fifteen to twenty miles from Ohio City. He wouldn't want me to coddle him—I'd already learned that the hard way—and no chance I wanted him to shut down on me.

**Let's look at the bus route tonight. That's always an option.**

What I wanted to suggest was him staying with me when he was on shift so I could drive him. But that was exactly the sort of thing he didn't want. That would feel too much like his arrangement with Michael, and West was anything if not fiercely independent. No way I'd want to extinguish that fire growing inside him. Besides, he'd only try to pay me like he did with Michael.

**Sounds good.**

Ever since the air show, we'd been seeing each other regularly. He'd either bike over, or I'd pick him up at his apartment, like I was doing tonight. But we were essentially on different schedules, so it only amounted to about three nights a week. Sundays definitely belonged to us since we were both off, and I cherished those days most of all.

It had turned out to be a beautiful fall with warmer temperatures, but it was still time for me to put the boat in storage for the winter, and I'd planned to do it week after next.

I also hadn't realized that West and Elijah had exchanged numbers that day on the boat during the air show, so a couple of times at work, Elijah would look down with a grin at something humorous West had texted.

"Your boy is funny," Elijah had said.

"I'm not sure he's my boy," I responded, rolling my eyes. "But yeah, he is."

"Oh, he's your boy all right," he said with a wink. "He mentions you every other sentence."

Damn if my heart didn't leap at that admission, even if Elijah was only yanking my chain.

At first, I'd admit I was jealous, wondering if West found Elijah attractive. At twenty-six, Elijah was definitely closer to his age. But then I got over myself, acknowledging that West needed friends in his life as much as anyone else and I couldn't begrudge him that.

When I pulled up to the curb, I wasn't sure if West was going to run out or I'd actually get to the door this time.

After he didn't come out right away, I walked up the steps to the porch and knocked. His roommate Marco answered the door and grinned at me, no doubt remembering the night from the club.

"West wanted me to tell you he's running late."

"No worries," I replied as he stepped aside to let me in.

West had worked the lunch shift at the restaurant, so he must've gotten caught up with errands afterward.

On the couch were Marco's brother, Angelo, and a pretty girl with dark hair, who was practically sitting on his lap. They greeted me distractedly as Angelo continued his assault on her neck, and I was having trouble looking anywhere else.

I walked to the opposite end of the room and focused on the apartment. The kitchen was off to the side with a worn table and chairs, and the furniture in the living room was mismatched and threadbare, which sort of reminded me of my first apartment on the college campus at Kent State.

Marco and I made small talk until West emerged from the shower and rushed to his room. "Sorry I'm late."

"Take your time," I replied with a smile as my pulse climbed a notch at seeing him. "We're not on a schedule."

West ushered me into his room, which contained a single bed and dresser.

His gaze swept over the room, as if seeing it for the first time through my eyes, and red dots formed on his cheeks. "I know it's not—"

"Don't. You know those things don't matter to me," I replied, pushing a stray strand of hair behind his ear. "Thank you for letting me come inside this time. For trusting me enough."

"You're welcome," he replied with a shiver as he stepped closer to me. I kissed a freckle on his bare shoulder before winding my fingers in his hair and pulling him into a kiss. He pushed his tongue inside my mouth with a moan as our lips and groins merged. We only had a damp towel between us, but I could feel his shaft plumping against my thigh.

"I like having you here," he said against my mouth. "Even though this is a crappy apartment."

I shrugged, kissing his cheek. "We all have to start somewhere."

"You always have the perfect thing to say," he remarked as he drew back and reached inside his dresser drawer for a clean pair of jeans and a gray T-shirt. He'd confessed during a late-night phone call that he'd had to purchase all his clothes from a secondhand shop, as if that was something to be ashamed of, and I told him as much, reminding him that I lived off foster-siblings' cast-offs my entire childhood. But he always looked adorably put-together to me.

I sat on his bed and looked my fill as he got dressed. Damn, he was gorgeous, all that smooth skin over lean muscle. As he fussed with his hair in the mirror, I spotted his hoodie hanging from the doorknob, and it reminded me of all those months back when I crushed on this guy I'd only get glimpses of through a car window.

Glancing down at his white pillow and soft blue comforter, I replayed all our conversations over the past few weeks and couldn't help smiling.

"Did you have to stay late at work?" I asked after he slid his wallet into his back pocket.

He turned an animated gaze toward me and shook his head. "Tony gave me a ride over to the Westlake restaurant to meet Chef Leanne."

He seemed so excited, I couldn't help reaching for him to pull him onto my lap. "Whoa, very cool. And?"

"The place is really nice. They're just getting it up and running and should be opening in another month." He bit his lip in apprehension. "But...I told her I didn't have transportation and that I was working on it."

"Good," I replied. "Leaving yourself open to the possibility."

"Right," he agreed and then suddenly cupped my jaw. "Thank you...for not trying to..."

"Of course," I replied and pecked him on the lips.

He wound his arms around my neck, and I breathed him in—rosemary and soap and West. My pulse calmed down and beat a steadier rhythm in my chest.

"So there's a new Thai restaurant in Tremont," I said against his neck. "Want to eat there?"

West drew back and frowned.

I arched a brow. "You don't like Thai food? That's cool."

"I love Thai. It's just that Tremont is a place..." He shook his head.

Then it dawned on me. "It's a place Michael would go?"

Tremont was a trendy, refurbished neighborhood a few blocks down from here that had several upscale restaurants, so that didn't surprise me. But it also explained why West chose not to apply for restaurant jobs in that area.

"Exactly," he replied with a nod. "He likes that area and had lots of business dinners there."

"I hate that you keep avoiding places," I pronounced, letting my frustration rear its ugly head. This topic kept cropping back up between us. "Damn it, West. What's the worst that could happen if he sees you living your life?"

"Dunno," he replied, finding his footing on the floor and taking a step back. "The idea of having to hash through shit with him... It's still too raw and uncomfortable to think about."

"Christ, I know it'll be awkward, but someday it'll happen, and you're going to have to face him and tell him some hard truths. You're being so headstrong about this, and I—"

"I'm not doing this with you right now." He stomped toward the door, and I immediately regretted letting my emotions get the best of me. He'd just thanked me in so many words for not involving myself in his decision-making, and here I was, practically lecturing him. *Fuck.*

Before he could get any farther, I reached for him, wound my arms around his torso, and pulled him tightly against me. "I'm sorry. I don't have the right... It's none of my business."

His resistance was only temporary before he melted against me.

"Why are you always so levelheaded about everything?" he ground out, and I could feel him trembling. "Don't you ever avoid shit that feels too big to deal with?"

"Are you kidding me? Do you know how many times I tried to avoid the hard things after Chris was gone?" I confessed against his ear. "All the paperwork in his name, his stuff jammed in every drawer in the condo. But it was no use; I had to face it."

"Well, maybe. I'm just not ready!" He tried to break away from me, but it was a weak effort.

"Okay, I get it." I placed my lips against his neck and inhaled him. "We don't have to bring it up again."

He spun in my arms to look at me.

"You don't get to call me on shit. I never expected this to happen with you...me..." He motioned between us. "Not when I was trying to—"

"I know," I replied, backing away. "The timing is awful, and I never want to be the reason you feel crowded again. I fucked up. I can totally leave—"

"Wait, that's not what I'm—" His shoulders deflated, and he shook his head. "It's just... You challenge me, make me question things...*feel* things."

My pulse beat steadily against my neck. "You make me feel things too."

He bit his lip as he worked through his thoughts. "Those feelings scare me."

I held his gaze. "Me too."

It somehow seemed like we'd found common ground again.

Finally, he cracked a smile, and I felt like I could breathe again. "Can we still eat somewhere—other than Tremont—because I'm starving."

I reached tentatively for his hand, and he wound our fingers together. "I'd love to. Let's go."

## 28

# WEST

I HAD A COUPLE OF HOURS LEFT OF MY SHIFT, AND I COULDN'T WAIT to go home and chill. Ever since Tristan and I had it out yesterday, things between us felt strange. We'd gone on to have a great meal, but something still felt off.

When he dropped me off, we clung to each other, both obviously sorry about the disagreement. I knew I was probably being unreasonable, but I just wanted a little more time. Things felt turned upside down in the months since I walked away from Michael. In a good way, sure, but overwhelming all the same.

And even though Tristan always gave me space, he challenged me too, and that was not necessarily a bad thing. In fact, he made me want to become a better version of myself.

We hadn't spoken since last night, but that wasn't unusual either. If I knew him by now, he was allowing me the time and distance to think things through.

I was bussing a table near the kitchen when I heard a new group of men being seated at the four-top by the window. When I glanced over, the hair on the back of my neck stood up.

*Michael.*

And from the looks of it, he was entertaining new clients.

My heart was hammering and my palms were clammy as I tried to get ahold of my runaway emotions. Why the hell was he dining in my restaurant?

I took my time replacing the silverware at the table as I worked to swallow the boulder in my throat and also so that the other busboy on shift would be responsible for greeting Michael's table first and filling their water glasses.

The next time I looked over, Michael was watching me, his eyes blown wide, his jaw ticking. He seemed just as stunned as me. I knew he wouldn't acknowledge me—a busboy—in front of his wealthy clients, so I was at least safe for the moment while I thought of any way at all not to have to be in contact with him.

Back at the server station, I watched him for a moment. Same expensive suit, perfectly coiffed hair. *I used to kiss that mouth*, I thought, and suddenly my stomach pitched. Michael was wound so tightly with my past that it was hard to see any flowers through all the weeds. Had he really gone from caretaker to lover in the span of a few years' time? Had I really let him fold me so seamlessly into his life?

I felt removed from him now, so starkly different and changed, it didn't even seem possible. It was remarkable what time and perspective could do.

"You okay?" George, the other busboy, asked.

"Yeah, just not feeling that great," I replied, which was a lie but also the truth. I felt nauseated and apprehensive all at once.

"No worries," George said. "I got this. Just a bunch of stuffy guys at that new table in the corner. Bet they'll stiff us on a tip anyway."

"Cool, thanks," I said, breathing out in relief. "Going to use the restroom real quick."

I walked down the short hall to the bathroom, splashed water on my face, and glanced in the mirror. I thought of Tristan's probing questions last night about what I might do if I ended up running into Michael, and fuck, it was as if our conversation had conjured him or something. Forcing me to get my head out of my ass.

I considered texting Tristan for moral support, then thought better of it. I was an adult and could handle a run-in with the ex. I was strong and had faced much worse in my life, for Christ's sake. This man was not going to influence me in any way, shape, or form. Not anymore.

When I exited the restroom, Michael stood waiting for me in the hallway, and the taste of bile crawled up my throat. Damn it. Though it made sense he'd seek me out away from prying eyes. I squared my shoulders. It was time to face him head-on.

"Jonas," he said upon seeing me, and I flinched hearing him use my real name. It'd been months.

"What are you doing here, of all places?" I asked.

"I could ask you the same thing. A busboy in a trendy restaurant? Seriously?" he asked in an accusing tone.

"Have you not been paying attention this whole time?" I balled my fists and seethed. "You thumbed your nose at my aspirations, thinking you knew better than me."

"You had a perfectly good job with decent pay," he threw back. "I was going to help you—"

"This is what I want to do with my life," I ground out. "You knew I took an interest in cooking, and you discouraged me at every turn."

"Really, you're going to pin that on me?" he scoffed. "Bussing tables isn't exactly culinary cuisine."

"You've got to start somewhere," I responded, using Tristan's catchphrase, and somehow it bolstered me. "I'm happy, Michael. Happier than I've been in years."

His jaw ticked. I had hurt his feelings, but I needed to be honest.

"Look, you were in my life during a time I really needed you, and I will eternally be grateful," I explained, and he relaxed his stance. "But now I'm trying to build something of my own. And I just want to be left alone. *Please*, don't make this any harder than it already is."

"You're not thinking straight," he said, lowering his voice and clutching my shoulder, but I shrugged him off. "Come back home and figure it out from there—even if you still want to...work *here*. I boxed up your things and kept them in your room just in case—"

"No," I said, more forcefully, panic gripping my throat. The very thought of returning to his condo made my stomach turn. There was nothing of value left for me anymore. "Leave me the hell alone. Go back to your clients."

When I stormed away from him, he didn't follow—he cared more about appearances, after all. Instead he calmly walked back to his clients as if he didn't just try to coax his ex-lover back home.

Back at the server station, George gave me the once-over. "You feeling better?"

I shrugged. "A little."

Avoiding eye contact with Michael again, I performed my duties in a daze all through dinner, simply begging for my shift to finally be over. Just hearing Michael's self-important voice and insincere laughter as he sweet-talked his clients was enough to last me a lifetime. As I was removing an extra place setting from a nearby table, I heard his voice ring out.

"Hey, busboy." My back stiffened. I kept walking, pretending I didn't hear him. "We need service over here."

I clenched my jaw as I turned toward the table and met his gaze. Michael was nothing if not proud, but his eyes gave him away—he was frustrated and a bit desperate as well. "Our water glasses need refilling."

He smirked at his clients. One gentleman snickered; the other appeared uncomfortable as he threw me a conciliatory glance. "Sure, let me grab the pitcher."

My hands trembled as I reached for the full decanter at the server station and walked it over to his table. George was replacing silverware at a table near the door, so I couldn't signal for him to take over. Except, I knew this was Michael's way of getting a dig in while forcing me to pay him attention. It infuriated me not only that I'd stayed under his thumb for so long, but that he felt so entitled in this situation.

But then I heard Tristan's calming tempo in my head. *Take it easy on yourself.*

"That's more like it," Michael muttered in a low tone as I bent over the table to fill the glasses. When his fingers reached out to brush against my elbow, that was more than I could take.

"Don't be an asshole," I growled in his direction. Clenching my jaw, I jerked the pitcher a few inches away from his glass, angling it just enough to dump the entire contents in his lap.

Michael jumped up in shock, practically tipping the table over in his haste. "Holy fuck, what the hell?"

"My bad," I replied, backing away. "I'll grab some towels."

I strode back to the service station, feeling a strange satisfaction in my chest, only to be confronted by my manager. "What the hell happened? You'll need to comp his bill and offer that gentleman dry cleaning on the house."

Fuck, I had created a scene, and this whole scenario was messing with my job—a job I had taken pride in. This little indiscretion was sure to come out of my tip earnings for the night.

"I apologize," I replied, pushing the towels into George's hands as the floor tilted at a nauseating angle. "I'm not feeling well."

Palm over my mouth, I strode through the kitchen straight outside to the Dumpster. Hands on my knees, I bent over and dry-heaved on the asphalt. I felt fucking humiliated.

Goddamn it. Now the offer to work at the other restaurant would probably be rescinded. With shaky fingers, I unchained my bike and climbed on, reiterating to the server who'd come out right then for a smoke break that I was sick and needed to leave.

Not waiting for a reply, I began pedaling away from the

restaurant, my breaths evening out the farther away I rode. When I got near the entrance to the alleyway, I heard the chain pop on the damn bike again. Fuck. I used my legs to come to a stop, my gaze swinging toward the back end, considering my options.

That was why I didn't notice the car pulling into the small driveway, and it was dark enough that the driver didn't see me on the bike either.

The impact was sudden as his bumper smashed into my front tire before he slammed on the brakes. Thankfully he wasn't traveling at a high speed. But it was enough of a jolt that I went careening over the top of my bike and landed on the pavement with a thud. My hands and knees took the brunt of the fall. As did my phone. It lay beside me smashed from the impact.

The driver burst from his door and squatted down beside me. "I'm so sorry. Are you okay?"

As I rose to my knees and straightened, I glanced down at myself, taking inventory. I felt the sting in my palms from road rash and a jolt of pain in my left knee. It was probably just bruised.

"I think I'm okay," I replied to the older man, whose face was stricken with guilt as much as fear. "Probably my fault; I wasn't paying attention to traffic."

I reached for my busted phone, the face smashed to pieces, bits of the screen lying on the sidewalk.

"What can I do?" the man asked, helping me to my feet. "Can I drive you home?"

I tensed, which I realized had become a programmed reaction. "Nah, I live just right around the corner. I'll be fine."

He reached for his wallet. "Please let me at least pay for the bike."

Before I knew what was happening, he was pulling out five twenty-dollar bills and forcing them into my skinned and sore hand. "It's better than the insurance or the cops getting involved."

I looked down at the wad of cash, dumbfounded. "Yeah, sure."

After he drove away, I tried to move my bike, but it was inoperable, so I left it propped against the building and limped the rest of the way home, my kneecap throbbing like it was on fire. I should've let the fucking guy drive me home. I was making so many shit decisions tonight and was beyond pissed at myself.

"What the hell happened to you?" Marco asked from the couch when I hobbled inside.

"Someone hit my bike; the front tire's all fucked up. And my knee."

After I explained where I left my bike, he threw aside the controller and stood up.

"Let's get your bike, and then I'll drive you to the clinic to get your knee checked out."

"I think my knee will be fine." I certainly didn't want to spend the money on an urgent care visit if I didn't have to. "Just want to retrieve my bike."

We slid in his car and headed back toward the restaurant. When he pulled up to the alleyway where I'd left my mangled bike, it was gone.

"What the actual fuck?" I said, pounding the dashboard, my gaze darting up and down the street.

"It would still be good for parts," Marco responded, wincing. "Even with a messed-up tire frame."

"Just fucking great," I grunted and threw my head back.

A stolen bike, a broken phone, a bruised knee, and possibly out of a job. Or at least disciplined for leaving work without permission—after spilling an entire pitcher of ice water on a customer.

And all for what? Because that fucker decided to show up at my job and I've been too much of a chickenshit to confront him sooner. Life sure had a way of pounding you over the head to make you pay attention to stuff you've deliberately missed.

## 29

# TRISTAN

AFTER I FINISHED CLIPPING THE BULLDOG'S NAILS AND SENT HIM over to the day-care side to play, I stared down at my phone again. No word from West in thirty-six hours.

Nervous that I overstepped my bounds the other night, I tried reaching out to him, but it went directly to voice mail. So unless he was sick or his phone had run out of battery, the only other thing I could gather was that he didn't want to talk to me. And even though in the back of my mind I was afraid this would happen, that West would try to disappear again, the reality of it was so much worse.

My chest felt like a gigantic weight was sitting on it, and I could scarcely breathe as I moved through my day in a fog.

Calling the restaurant made me feel like I was checking up on him, so after they told me he wasn't on the schedule for the next couple of days, I didn't try to do anything stupid like show up at his place. I wasn't going to breathe down his neck like Michael would've. I might've felt desperate and a bit wrecked, but I was not going to become that person.

All I could do was try to look on the bright side. West had

reawakened something inside me, made me feel hopeful again these last few months, and I'd always remember that.

I fingered the silver chain around my neck; I'd found it in the junk drawer last night—the one forgotten place I hadn't organized in years. It was my first gift from Chris after college graduation, and I used to wear it religiously. Feeling its cool surface now brought me some level of comfort.

*I can get through this too. Right, Chris?*

*I was making room for him in my heart, but maybe I shouldn't have. Maybe neither of us was ready for that.*

Mack nudged his nose at my knees, so I scooped him up on the table and rubbed behind his ears just the way he liked. "You feeling needy too, buddy?"

My shoulders sagged as I looked down at my phone one last time before sliding it in my back pocket.

Elijah thumped my shoulder. "He's not responding to my texts either."

My stomach lurched, hoping West wasn't sick or in any kind of trouble. Maybe I'd drive by his apartment after work just to make sure.

"Not a good idea," I mumbled to myself as I placed Mack back down on the ground and headed for the computer to respond to a couple of suppliers.

"Just give West some space, and he'll come around," Elijah suggested, and Brin muttered in agreement as he reached for a leash to use on the day-care side.

I nodded, but I wasn't convinced.

"Is Stewart giving *you* space?" I asked. Elijah was at least looking more rested, like maybe he was getting some sleep.

"Nope," Brin said, answering for him from the doorway. "He shows up at the apartment for booty calls."

"I'm going to kill Nick for blabbing everything to you," Elijah whined.

"He's just worried about you," Brin retorted. "We all are."

"I know," Elijah replied with a sigh. "Stewart just looks so pathetic and miserable without me."

Brin shook his head. "You'll never know if you're better off without him if you don't give yourself enough time to figure it out."

"What Brin said," I added as I sat down at the desk.

I wasn't going to do that to West. He had my number, he knew where I lived and worked, and I'd give him the time he needed. Having made up my mind, I powered through the rest of my day.

But later that night, doubt began creeping in again.

I pulled out my cell as I lay in bed with Mack at my feet.

*I miss holding you.*

*I think I love you.* My heart lodged in my throat. *Fuck.*

Instead I typed, **If you need me, you know where to find me.**

---

THE FOLLOWING MORNING THE PHONE RANG AT DOGGIE STYLES, and I grumbled at the shrill sound, not having had my fill of coffee yet. Plus, I slept like shit.

Still, I lifted the receiver and forced out a greeting in a cheerful voice.

"Somebody hocked your shitty bike."

I inhaled a sharp breath, feeling a hundred times better just hearing West's voice.

"Eh, suppose it was only a matter of time."

When he chuckled into the phone, my shoulders unwound further. Damn, I missed that laugh.

"It's good to hear your voice," I said tentatively. I reached for my coffee mug to pour myself a refill.

"I'm using Marco's cell. Mine is totally busted—along with everything else it seems."

"What the hell does that mean?" I asked, my voice spiked with concern, the cup nearly slipping from my fingers.

"Well, your bike got wrecked before it was snagged...and also my knee."

I gripped the counter, kicking myself for not listening to my intuition. Something had definitely felt off the past couple of days. "Holy shit, what happened?"

He recounted the events from a couple of nights back when Michael showed up at his restaurant and followed him to the bathroom to try to strong-arm him into coming home. Apparently, West had dumped water on him after Michael embarrassed him at the table; then he took off on the bike, and somebody smashed his tire.

It didn't sound like anything got resolved with Michael, but I held my tongue, done with offering advice unless he asked for it. But man, I was half tempted to find Michael myself and give him a piece of my mind.

"That's definitely a shit couple of days," I said with some awe. "What did your manager end up saying?"

"He was pretty cool about it," he replied, and there was relief in his tone. "Said I'd never pulled that shit before, so he's giving me the benefit of the doubt."

"Awesome." I blew out a breath. I would've been bummed had he lost his job. "What's up with your knee?"

"Sprain," he replied with a grumble. "Doc said to keep it iced and elevated and it should feel better in a couple of days."

"That why you're off work?" I asked without thinking.

"How did you—"

I winced.

"Was worried. Elijah too," I replied. "Sorry, wasn't trying to pry."

"It's cool," he replied. "I appreciate the concern."

"Honestly, I wasn't sure... The other night when we argued—"

"You were right...about Michael," he breathed out.

"I wasn't right to push you." I shook my head even though he couldn't see it. "That wasn't fair."

"That's what friends do, right?"

*Friends.* That was the only thing we were, and this conversation was a needed reminder. Didn't matter if sex had become part of the equation, or emotions—we both knew the risks, and I couldn't begrudge him that.

I attempted to keep a level voice. "Yeah...yeah, sure."

"So, I, um...need to return Marco's cell. Going to worry about getting a new phone this weekend." There was a moment's hesitation before he said the words I knew were coming. "I obviously need to work some shit out. Seeing Michael shouldn't have sent me into such a tailspin."

"Take all the time you need," I said around a thick throat. "It's your life after all. It'll be important to figure out what you want."

"And what I need?" he added in a soft voice.

My heart choked off my airway. "Absolutely."

It sounded so final. But the truth was, I had been caught up in this whirlwind with him, and even though I gave him the illusion of time and space, he had plenty to figure out on his own about his past as well as his future.

I wanted him to promise me that we'd stay in contact, but that would've been pretty selfish. It was better he worked things through on his own.

"So...guess I'll catch you later," West said, sounding a tad sad and defeated. And though that gave me a bit of hope that this parting was just as hard on him, it was best not to prolong this conversation, lest one of us said something we'd regret.

"If you ever need anything, you know where to find me." I attempted to sound more jovial, even though my heart was sitting like dead weight in my gut.

"Th-thanks," he replied unsteadily.

"And, West? For what it's worth, the last few months have been...some of my favorites."

# 30

# WEST

By the weekend, I had made up my mind. I was going to Michael's place. Maybe if I showed up at his condo and grabbed a box of my stuff, we could finally get some closure. I understood now why it was important. I had left him on a whim, when the moment presented itself. I was hoping to avoid a melodramatic farewell—but now I needed to face it head-on.

That final phone conversation with Tristan had left me feeling raw and exposed. Goodbyes were tough for me in general—I'd had too many of them in my short life, and he was someone I couldn't bear to say those words to.

*For what it's worth, the last few months have been...some of my favorites.*

*Fuck, Tristan. How do you always say the most perfect things?*

As it stood, I missed him something fierce, but if I hoped to someday count him as a friend, I needed to learn how to become a better one first. And that could only be accomplished by stepping up, being mature about my decisions, and taking ownership of my actions and feelings.

I hobbled to Marco's car, the swelling in my knee having gone down, but I needed an extra day or two before I'd feel comfortable enough to get behind the wheel of someone else's car. He'd agreed to drive me to my former condo and wait for me in the lot.

My fingers shook as I knocked on Michael's condo door. I could've used my key, but I decided to return it to him instead. That might help solidify the message that we were over.

When he pulled open the door, shock registered on his face before he reeled it in. Coco and Chloe bounded from somewhere behind him, yipping excitedly at me. I bent over to rub them behind the ears and beneath their chins, feeling momentarily shaken seeing them again. They looked as healthy and exuberant as ever, and I knew Michael had taken good care of them.

"What are you doing here?" he asked, taking in my appearance. I made sure not to favor my bad knee. He didn't need to know I was hurt. If he was still angry about the water incident at his table, he certainly didn't show it.

Instead, his eyes lit up in anticipation. "Does this mean you..."

"No," I said, wanting to make it obvious immediately. "I came to pick up my things...so we can both move on."

When my gaze leveled on his, there was uncertainty mixed with anger and sadness in his eyes. He finally nodded and allowed me to step inside.

From a quick cursory glance, everything looked the same—plush couches and rugs, stainless-steel appliances, top-of-the-line furniture—and yet it seemed surreal that I had ever lived here with him to begin with. I had few possessions that belonged to me outright besides my clothes—any games, movies, or music were always borrowed from his vast collection—so I couldn't imagine this visit would take longer than a few minutes.

"Maybe if we talk it through—" he began, but I cut him off at the pass.

"Don't you think I would've showed up sooner if I wanted that?"

His jaw ticked in frustration.

"If you dug down deep, you could probably admit to yourself

that you and I never really worked." I took a deep breath and said exactly what I was thinking. "We were probably just...a convenience to each other, you know?"

He shook his head in exasperation. "Did you ever...care for me at all?"

"Yes, of course. In my own way. You helped me through some tough times." He breathed out, visibly relieved. "But the way you treated me the other night? That kind of shit chips away at any warm feelings I had."

I folded my arms, feeling emboldened. Getting it all out in the open felt freeing, like I was being unburdened. "You were a self-righteous ass to me at my place of employment, and I deserve an apology."

He narrowed his eyes. "I deserve an apology for the way you walked out on me."

We stared each other down, but I didn't want to drag this out.

"You're right," I replied, and his eyes widened a fraction. "That wasn't cool of me. But it almost felt like I had no choice. You can be stubborn, overbearing... Can you at least admit to that?"

"Okay, fine," he ground out. "But you walked away like it was nothing, and I...I was...*worried* about you."

I sighed. I supposed I didn't expect him to actually say he was *hurt* by me. He had too much pride for that. What the hell did I expect? Miracles?

"That was why I asked Tristan to pass on the message that I was okay. I know I should've done it myself, but at the time—"

"Yeah, *that* guy. He—"

"Don't. Tristan is a good man." I rushed my hands through my hair in frustration. "Fuck, Michael, why does everything have to come down to status and money? That's not all there is in life."

"Those things can work to your advantage," he argued.

I so didn't want to hear another lecture about wealth and influence. "Listen, I know you only wanted the best for me, but

I'm not you. I'm not for you either, but there probably is someone out there who is."

When I dug inside my pocket and handed him back the key to his condo, he looked bewildered, but I couldn't find it in me to feel bad for him. He'd make it on his own just fine.

"And honestly, since you already have them in boxes, you can just donate my clothes to charity," I said as his gaze scanned over my secondhand jeans and shoes. Screw him. These clothes finally felt like me, and I was actually cool wearing them.

"Take care, Michael." I turned toward the doorway, trying like hell not to hobble so I could make a gracious exit with my dignity intact.

"Jonas, wait." I froze at the sound of my name. I almost asked him to call me West, but that wouldn't sound right coming from him.

"I have something for you," he said, and when I turned, he held up a finger. He strode down the hall toward my old room with the pugs in tow, and I was left wondering what in the hell could he possibly be retrieving.

He reentered the living room, carrying a medium-sized box.

"What's that?"

"I think..." He swallowed thickly as his eyes met mine. "Serena had stored this in the crawl space. It was dropped off by the social worker one day while you were at school. She'd intended to show you at a later date, but then I guess time just got away from us."

I could feel my hands trembling and my pulse pounding in my ears.

*Just grab the box and get the hell out of there.*

I stepped forward and fished it from his arms.

"Thank you, Michael," I said in a level voice.

When I got to the hallway, he said, "One more thing."

He pulled an envelope out of his pocket.

"What's that?"

"I...saved all the money you gave me over the years."

I shook my head. "I don't want it."

"*Please,* take it," he insisted, placing the envelope on top of the box. "I know you can use it."

"Why are you doing this?" I ground out, feeling overwhelmed and on edge.

"Guess I'm trying to apologize in my own way," he replied in a solemn voice. "And show you that I...I can respect your decision."

I backed away from him toward the elevators, feeling equal parts relieved and anxious. "That'll remain to be seen."

---

WHEN I GOT HOME, I LOCKED MYSELF IN MY ROOM AND PACED THE floor, working up the nerve to open the box comprised of memories from my past. I knew it contained things left over from the fire, and I didn't know if I could bear to go through it.

*You have to face it.*

My fingers shook as I cautiously opened the lid. The acrid smell of smoke nearly made me gag. My eyes stung and my throat ached as I pulled out one of the twins' teddy bears, the fur slightly charred.

Gulping in air, I lifted two of my grandmother's favorite bird figurines from the box, and four blue dinner plates from my mother's favorite set. I was amazed they had survived the flames unscathed. I could picture each so perfectly, their places prominent in my grandmother's curio case in the dining room.

Arranging each item around me on the mattress, I sank down on my sheets, clutching the bear to my chest, and sobbed until there were no more tears left to give.

## 31

# TRISTAN

It was a chilly fall day, and the crisp wind whipping off Lake Erie made the task of securing the boat cover a bear. This chore was supposed to have been completed last weekend, but I made every excuse not to come, now that West's memory was also tied to this place. But it was practically deserted here, and I didn't want to put it off any longer.

Having an entire season away would do me good. I'd be ready to start fresh next spring and hopefully create some new memories.

Or maybe I'd just sell her.

As soon as I finished securing the last of the snaps near the bow, the marina would handle the rest. I had already paid for the storage space in their warehouse.

"She gave us a good summer, didn't she?" a voice called from the dock.

I'd been so lost in my task, I hadn't heard my visitor approach. I closed my eyes momentarily, trying to steady my runaway pulse.

"One of the best summers I ever had," I replied around a tight throat.

When I turned, West stood on the dock, wearing a worn

herringbone tweed coat pushed up at the elbows. It lent him a more sophisticated air than his hoodie ever did, but he looked adorable either way.

And fuck if he didn't take my breath away every single time.

"Me too," he replied, making my pulse quicken as our gazes clashed. He looked away as he self-consciously toed the seam of a wooden slat. "So...I, uh, replaced your bike with an equally shitty one."

I searched around the dock, wondering what in the world he meant.

He motioned with his thumb over his shoulder. "It's in the back seat of my clunker."

My eyes snapped to his. "A car?"

"Yeah," he responded with a sheepish grin. "It's a long story, but I was able to put a down payment on a used Honda. Hopefully it won't die on me anytime soon."

My eyebrow arched. "I look forward to hearing this story."

He grinned as his cheeks grew rosy. "The bike isn't a direct match, but Kam helped me choose something pretty close."

I shook my head. "You didn't have to—"

"Yeah, I did. I owed you. For so many things," he muttered.

When he stepped closer, my heart lurched. He was so beautiful, my fingers itched to reach out. I carefully climbed toward the foothold and stepped onto the dock to meet him halfway.

I could see his pulse pounding in his throat as I took him in—his deep eyes, long lashes, full lips. His coat was frayed around the buttonholes, and I pondered if he'd bought it from the same secondhand shop. It had character and charm, just like him.

"Elijah told me you'd be here."

"Yeah?" I asked as I recalled the random text from him this morning asking what my day looked like. Sneaky bastard.

"I'm considering renting a room from him now that Nick moved out."

I blinked, trying to take that information in. West was going to be living closer. Did that mean…

"And in a couple of weeks, I'm going to be starting as a kitchen assistant at the new location."

I reached for him, unable to stop myself from clutching his shoulder. "I'm happy for you."

"Thanks," he replied and then stiffened briefly as he seized my hand. "Where's your wedding band?"

His eyebrows knit together as he studied my eyes.

"It was time." I shrugged as if it was no big thing when we both knew damn well it was huge. My fingers fumbled for the chain around my neck as I fished it out. "Guess we match."

The color on his cheeks darkened, and it sort of felt like that first time he showed up at the boat. Shy glances giving way to longing looks as the electric current that always tethered us together sparked in intensity, drawing us closer.

But I still didn't know why he'd come. Was it to get closure with me as well?

The thought sat like a heavy lump in my stomach.

"I, uh, still owe you a bunch of dinners too," West said, glancing at me from under his lashes. "But I wasn't sure if you'd still—"

"I'll always want to spend time with you," I replied with conviction in my voice.

His breath hitched as his eyes fixed on mine.

"But I wouldn't want you to feel…" I shook my head, my heart thundering in my ears. "Obligated or tied down."

"You never tied me down. You always set me free."

His smile was brilliant as his gaze filled with affection.

I couldn't draw in air fast enough, as my pulse jackhammered in my veins and all of my dulled senses seemed to reawaken.

"I want to be with you, Tristan," West said in a thick voice. He knotted our fingers together and took a deep breath as his lips trembled. "I'm madly in love with you."

*Holy fuck.* My heart ballooned in my chest as I bent forward to brush our mouths together. "I'm in love with you too."

He closed his eyes and leaned his forehead against mine. "I missed you like crazy."

"Tell me about it." We stayed that way, simply breathing the same sliver of air between us, bringing our mouths and tongues together in gentle kisses.

I drew away to make sure we were still alone on the dock. "Let me finish the last of the snaps."

He waited on the dock, glancing out at the water past the breakwall. "I'll miss these Sundays."

"There's always football season," I replied with a smirk. "I planned on watching today's game."

"Want some company?" His voice was filled with yearning, and I couldn't wait to get him alone so I could kiss him for longer. "I can give you the bike and tell you that story."

I arched a brow as I stepped away from the boat, satisfied that it was secured for the season. "Only if you plan to feed me."

We locked hands and began walking toward the parking lot. "You couldn't stop me even if you tried."

## 32

# WEST

I MADE TRISTAN DINNER AS OFTEN AS I COULD, GIVEN OUR OPPOSING schedules. I suggested keeping my mother's blue plates in his cupboard so our meals could be served on them whenever possible. He loved the idea, and it made our time together that much more special.

I was also learning a ton from Chef Leanne, but that meant I was on schedule most nights. We made it work, though. We cherished our days off and at least one evening a week, when I used my key to let myself inside his place so I could sleep with him.

I hadn't seen him in a couple of days, and I was practically thrumming with need. After shedding my clothes, I slipped inside the covers. When I finally felt his warm and naked skin against mine, I hummed in satisfaction.

"Mmmmm," he purred against my neck. "I've missed you."

His tender kisses always made me shiver.

"Missed you too," I whispered as Tristan flipped me onto my back and stared adoringly into my eyes.

"Fuck, you're beautiful. Are you really mine?" he murmured as his palm gripped the back of my head and he hauled me into an overwhelming kiss that made my bones turn liquid.

"Tristan, I..." Gasping, I broke the kiss. "I want... Tonight, can you..." I wrapped my legs around his thighs and jerked my hips upward. Tristan blinked, understanding finally dawning in his eyes as our stiff cocks aligned. "Please."

He pinned me to the bed, my wrists over my head, his lips on my mouth. "Are you sure?"

The need had been building inside me for days, and I'd only been brave enough to ask tonight. It felt perfect to be inside him during sex, but I wanted him to fill me too.

"Yes. Make love to me," I urged, wiggling against him. I thought I might die if I didn't finally get to feel his cock stretching me. "I know you haven't—"

His lips welded to mine, and his tongue pushed inside my mouth as he moaned and rubbed our cocks together. "Goddamn, West. I want you so bad."

He reached blindly for the lube and condoms on the nightstand, and I panted in anticipation as I heard him prepping himself.

He hovered over my body as he kissed my neck and then sucked a mark into my throat, making me shudder. Tristan pushed my knees toward my shoulders and circled my hole with this thumb as I squirmed impatiently against him.

"No," I whined. "Just fuck me. Need you inside."

He hesitated briefly before guiding his cock to line up with my hole. I could feel his thighs trembling, and I thought he might change his mind, tell me he wasn't ready.

I knew how huge this was for him, and my heart stuttered as I watched his eyes for any signs of uncertainty or distress. But all I saw was longing and affection that mirrored mine.

"You make me so happy," he whispered, kissing my temple.

His gaze was hungry with need as his tip brushed over the knotted ring of muscle, the blunt head of his cock resting on the cusp of penetration.

With a brusque breath, he pressed past the initial resistance, finally breaching me. He hissed as he ground in place, arching his head back and panting openly, his rib cage moving with effort. "So tight and...*fuck*."

My teeth clamped down because it burned, my muscles spasming as they spread to accommodate his girth, but I urged him forward with my heels, because it also felt fucking amazing.

"So good." The stretch and fullness were the exact thing I needed in this moment.

There was complete wonder in his gaze as his fingers traced over my lips and down my chin, making my stomach tingle, until finally he snapped his hips, prodding forward.

"Damn, that's—" He panted as he drove the last few inches inside.

Instinct taking over, he pumped in shallow bursts, clenching his jaw as he adjusted to the sensation.

Finding his rhythm, he thrust harder, providing the perfect friction against my prostate as my teeth ground together, my climax already barreling toward me.

"Oh fuck, yes," I sobbed, so close as he reached down to stroke my cock. I wound my hand over the top of his fingers to help jerk me off. He tweaked my nipples, intensifying my pleasure.

"Wait, not yet." I clutched at his wrists to still him as my vision grew spotty. "Damn, Tristan."

"I...I can't." He moaned loudly, his eyes blown wide and his jaw hanging open in bliss.

Just watching him find pleasure in our connection sent me over the edge. The room whited out as my orgasm ripped through me. I threw my head back and shouted his name.

Tristan grew motionless, either to let me ride out my orgasm or maybe to prolong the sensation. Then, pushing my thighs upward, he changed the angle and fucked down into me. He pumped hard several more times before he shuddered and spurted his load deep inside me.

"Fuck. *Fuck.*" Collapsing on top of me, he buried his face in my neck and inhaled me, the importance of what we'd done not lost on either of us.

He sucked on my neck while I wound my arms and legs tightly around him, never wanting to let go. He took my mouth, tangling our tongues together before feathering kisses down my chest to my groin, cleaning the come as he went.

I writhed beneath him because my skin felt tender, pinpricks still lining my arms and legs. When he licked at my slit and gave my cock a reverent kiss, I practically melted into the mattress.

Ripping off the condom, he deposited it in the trash can before sinking down in the sheets and engulfing me in his arms, my back to his chest.

"Th...thank you." His voice was rough, and a moment later I felt wetness at the side of my neck. "For...being you. For giving me that."

I whimpered, tugging at his arms so that I was completely encompassed by him as emotion clogged my throat.

The urge to turn and gaze at him, wipe his tears and kiss them away came over me. But I didn't want to interrupt this moment. This was about more than sex. This was about the last vestiges of grief. About saying goodbye.

I gently lifted his hand to my mouth. When I kissed his palm and the suntan line where his ring used to rest, a sob tore from his throat.

Locating the pulse point in my neck, I placed his fingers directly against it, knowing he needed that reassurance. That I was here in the flesh and I wasn't planning on going anywhere.

We had both lost people and understood the brutal fragility of life.

Tristan was making room for me in his heart, and I would never take that for granted.

When he breathed my name against my ear, I felt like I was

finally his to cherish. He was letting me in, letting me have all of him.

"I love you, Tristan...so fucking much."

---

SOMEBODY NEW WAS KNOCKING ON THE DOOR AT TRISTAN'S PLACE, just as I was pulling the last appetizer out of the oven.

"Glad you could make it," I heard Tristan say.

Brin and Nick were already cozy on the love seat, and Elijah and Kam were sitting on the floor in front of the coffee table, watching the first quarter of the Browns game.

From the sound of the voices I could tell that Judy and Sheri had arrived, and I stiffened briefly because I hadn't seen them since the air show.

They made themselves at home on the couch, and Tristan took drink orders while I placed the spinach and artichoke dip alongside the other appetizers on the table.

"This buffalo-chicken dip is to die for," Brin remarked before stuffing a tortilla chip in his mouth.

"West made all this stuff," Tristan replied with a smile. "I had no part in it."

"That's a good thing," Sheri commented with a smirk.

"Right?" Elijah winked. "I think you should keep him around."

"Oh, I plan on it," Tristan said, and I could feel a line of heat crawl across my neck. "If my cleanliness habits don't drive him away sooner."

Tristan tugged on my hand so I would sit down on the floor next to him. I hadn't taken a moment to myself since I started prepping a couple of hours ago. Mack waddled toward me and lay down at my feet. My hands naturally glided over his smooth fur. Brin had brought Tally, and she was currently seated near Nick's feet, hoping he'd drop some food.

I shot a nervous glance toward Judy and Sheri, who were smiling brightly at us.

I breathed out a sigh of relief. "Well, any place is bound to be cleaner than Elijah's bedroom."

"Right?" Nick said, leaning over and fist-bumping me.

"Shut it," Elijah said around a swallow of beer. "It's not that bad."

Brin chuckled. "Most days you can't even see the floor."

"Whatever," he grumbled, while Kam laughed and nudged his shoulder.

I'd moved into Elijah's place last weekend, and so far, so good. We got along great and seemed to agree on most things. As it was, Angelo's girlfriend had been staying over every single night, and it was feeling a bit crowded at my old apartment. I promised Marco I'd keep in touch, had even invited him to Tristan's place for the game today, but he was working the lunch shift.

I looked around at this lively bunch, people I now considered friends, finally feeling settled and more content than ever. My boyfriend was gorgeous and loving and supportive, and I was working toward a promising career. What more could I ask for?

Maybe someday, Tristan and I could share our lives in more intimate ways. I shivered at the prospect of eventually having a place of our own, but one thing at a time.

During a commercial break, I noticed how Judy's gaze tracked around the room and landed on the photo of Chris on the bookshelf. Beside it, Tristan had placed a picture he'd recently taken of me and Mack walking along the lake, and I bit my lip, wondering how that made her feel.

At halftime everyone got up to stretch, use the restroom, or to grab a fresh drink. Judy had stepped out onto the balcony, and for some reason I felt compelled to join her, if only to settle some of my anxieties. I'd gotten better at facing my fears head-on, but I was still a work in progress. Weren't we all.

"Isn't this view everything?" she said as if already sensing it was me.

"Yeah," I replied, staying near the door. "The fall leaves are gorgeous from up here."

"Come and sit," she said, motioning to the other chair across from the small table. "Tell me about that chain around your neck. Is that a mother's ring?"

She was trying to find common ground, and though it was a tender topic, I appreciated it. So I did. I shared a couple of things about my family, and she told me a story about Chris and Tristan when they were barely legal. It felt like a start. Like we were getting to know each other better.

*They're my family too. They'll always be important to me.*

Tristan was suddenly at the door. "You're going to miss the second half."

When he threw a concerned glance in my direction, I offered him a lopsided grin, and he retreated back inside with a relieved nod.

"He's so happy," Judy remarked as she stood up and glanced one last time at the lake.

"I'm...happy too," I replied unsteadily. "Is that—"

"It's fantastic," she answered, beaming at me. "You both deserve it."

"Thank you." I glanced down, trying to rein in my wavering pulse.

As she slid open the balcony door, she said, "I hope you'll join us this Christmas in Port Clinton."

My eyes jerked to meet her steady gaze. "Th...thank you for inviting me. Tristan says it's pretty there."

She nodded and smiled.

"Chris would've loved you too," she whispered as she patted my shoulder and made her way inside.

I stood staring after her, my heart feeling like it was beating outside of my chest.

Tristan's thumb brushed beneath my chin. "You okay?"

"I'm perfect," I replied with a sigh.

"Yes, you are," he murmured against my ear. "Perfectly mine."

I shivered. "You're corny, old man."

"Old man, huh?" He cocked an eyebrow. "Just wait until I get you alone."

"I look forward to it," I replied with a wink.

After I refilled the chip bowls, Tristan pulled me to sit between his legs on the floor. When he folded me against him and planted a kiss at my temple, I sighed as a peaceful contentment spread inside my chest. I'd never felt more myself than in this man's arms.

## OTHER TITLES BY CHRISTINA LEE

*Male/Male Romance*

There You Stand

The Darkest Flame

The Faintest Spark

The Deepest Blue

The Hardest Fall

The Sweetest Goodbye

Co-written with Nyrae Dawn (AKA Riley Hart):

Touch the Sky

Chase the Sun

Paint the Stars

Living Out Loud

*Between Breaths Series (New Adult Romance)*

All of You

Before You Break

Whisper to Me

Promise Me This

There You Stand (m/m)

*Adult Contemporary Romance*

Two of Hearts

Three Sacred Words

Twelve Truths and a Lie

# ABOUT THE AUTHOR

Once upon a time, **Christina Lee** lived in New York City and was a wardrobe stylist. She spent her days getting in cabs, shopping for photo shoots, eating amazing food, and drinking coffee at her favorite hangouts.

Now she lives in the Midwest with her husband and son—her two favorite guys. She's been a clinical social worker and a special education teacher. But it wasn't until she wrote a weekly column for the local newspaper that she realized she could turn the fairy-tales inside her head into the reality of writing fiction.

She's addicted to lip balm, coffee, and kissing. Because everything is better with kissing.

She writes MM Contemporary as well as Adult and New Adult Romance. She believes in happily-ever-afters for all, so reading and writing romance for everybody under the rainbow helps quench her soul.

## ACKNOWLEDGMENTS

To the kid I read about in the newspaper who lost everyone in a fire. I had you in mind when writing West's character. I truly hope you finally found peace.

To Rob, for letting me borrow a couple details for Tristan. You are one of the coolest and strongest people I know and I hope you and A get your happily-ever-after.

To Greg and Jessie: For helping me navigate the world of boating, dining, and dog grooming.

To Michelle: Thanks for helping me organize my release and saving me from being a hot mess. You are a gem!

Riley, Keren, Dianne, Judy: Thank you for helping make the bones of my book strong and polished.

To Greg and Evan, for not complaining when I have to disappear to work at odd hours of any random day. I don't want to be in any other place in the world except right next to you, every single night.

To my family and friends for your constant, unwavering support. I love you.

To the amazing book bloggers and reviewers: please know that I appreciate all the work you do—all on your own dime—for the simple love of books.

To the readers: THANK YOU for taking a chance on my books and reaching out to talk to me about them. For an author, there may be no better feeling.

## 33

## AN EXCERPT FROM LIVING OUT LOUD

BEN

THE CURSOR BLINKS AS I CONSIDER WHETHER TO LEAVE WELL enough alone. My palms sweat as I begin typing the message, my fingers fumbling on the keys:

**Hey, Xavier! This is Ben Emerson. It's been a long time.**

*A long time since we were fourteen and shared a first kiss. A long time since I freaked, pushed you away, and barely spoke to you after that.*

*Your family moved the following year, and I never saw you again. Surprised I didn't search for you online sooner. But life's been rough, to say the least. And I've been scared for too damn long. And now I'm finally on my own....Trying to find my way in this vibrant city. Guess it feels nice to reach out to an old friend. Don't have too many of those anymore. Someone familiar in an overwhelming situation.*

I hit the back button and delete the short message. Exit out of Facebook and walk to the fridge to pull out a cold soda, glad my roommate isn't around to see me stress out like this over a damn social media message.

But lots of shit is new to me lately. Moving to San Fran, for example, and finally leaving my conservative family behind. I lift my ball cap and push my sweaty hair away from my eyes before readjusting it onto my head.

I have a little collection of hats now that I work outdoors for a landscaping business called Common Grounds. An assortment of thin cotton drawstring shorts and T-shirts too—the kind with the armholes cut out for extra air conditioning. They're the most comfortable when laying down fertilizer and spreading mulch in front of the quaint Victorian homes on Steiner Street, also known as Postcard Row or the Painted Ladies, depending on who you're speaking to in this town.

I left my Sunday best—those suffocating dress shirts, slacks, and ties—behind and became someone new. Someone who feels more like me and that's incredibly freeing. Like I'm finally breaking away from my minister father and his flock of followers. Standing in the front pew of the makeshift tent that eventually became a brick-and-mortar church for an entire childhood while he *saved* people with little more than bible verses and a fuckton of arrogance...as the congregation fell to their knees in prayer and thanked the almighty stars.

My mother was no different; she'd put the Tammy Faye Bakkers of the world to shame with her floral dresses and strings of pearls as she happily waved to the bible camp bus as it sped away with me and a dozen other kids inside it, only to find out later that she hoped I'd return more devout than ever. *As if I ever had a choice back then.*

Helping Dad keep the church books after graduation felt just as wrong—like I was only playing a role. Going through the motions, while my feelings were at war inside me. Putting my hands in the dirt felt much better and was familiar to me—God's green earth and all of that.

I glance at the clock and wonder what's taking Drew so long with our takeout order from the corner pizza place. Sitting back down on the stool, I reach for my laptop. I reopen Facebook, type in Xavier's name, and scroll through his photos again like some stalker.

First time I saw him as an adult, I nearly swallowed my tongue. Because hot damn, he's a sexy man. I've never thought that about somebody with a shit-ton of piercings and tattoos, but on him they look cool. His hair is still dark and wavy, though he wears it longer now. A mix of confidence and dreaminess still exudes from his eyes. Except now they're lined with black kohl, which makes the whiskey-brown color stand out. His skin is still a shade or two darker than mine, which he likely got from his father who is half Mexican.

There's no status listed beneath his photo, so it's hard to tell whether he's taken or single, not that it matters. But he's definitely openly gay if the rainbow flags and equality memes on his posts are any indication.

I enlarge a recent photo and notice his T-shirt for the first time. It reads, Weed Saves Lives. My heart squeezes uncomfortably tight. Damn, is he into that shit as hard as Ezra, my ex from college? Again, why does it matter? I'm not trying to date him, only reconnect with an old friend. But from the looks of it, we're different as night and day. I'm still shaking my bible-thumping traditional upbringing, and he's as free and eclectic as this town.

I hear a key scrape in the door as my roommate walks in, carrying our pizza. "Sorry, there was a line."

I shut my laptop and twist toward him. "No worries. Is Wendy joining us?"

"She had a work thing," he replies, placing the large box in the middle of the table as I reach for a couple of plates from the cupboard.

Drew and his fiancée, Wendy, have been so gracious since renting me this room four months ago. This is technically Drew's apartment, but they're engaged to be married and want to save money for all the expenses they'll be accruing next year. So Drew thought having a temporary roommate in an expensive city was the perfect idea. Over a couple of beers last month, Drew shared that Wendy still resides with her parents, who frown upon the idea of them living together before marriage, and since they're primarily footing the bill, they decided not to rock the boat.

"How was your day?" he asks around his slice of broccoli and mushroom. Not my favorite combo but since he's a vegetarian and has been so cool with helping me navigate this city, I'm not going to complain. There are plenty more eye-opening things to embrace besides veggies on a pizza.

I briefly tell him about the flower garden we planted today with the plastic pink flamingos in Nob Hill and he fills me in on his busy day as a programmer in Silicon Valley.

Once we obliterate the pizza, Drew's cell rings with a call from Wendy and he heads to his room to talk to her in private. Alone with my thoughts again, I take a deep breath to bolster my courage, open my laptop, and tell myself I've got nothing to lose.

**Hey, Xavier! This is Ben Emerson. It's been a long time. I heard through the grapevine that you live in the city and I recently moved here too. Just wanted to say hi and that I'm sorry...about a lot of things. Hope all is cool on your end.**

I hit send and hope like hell he isn't still holding a ten-year grudge.

Made in the USA
Columbia, SC
08 January 2018